Princess Candy

THE EVIL ECHO

STONE ARCH BOOKS
a capstone imprint

PRINCESS CANDY
THE EVIL ECHO

WRITTEN BY

MICHAEL DAHL & SCOTT NICKEL

ILLUSTRATED BY

JEFF CROWTHER

DESIGNER: **BRANN GARVEY**

EDITOR: **JULIE GASSMAN**

EDITORIAL DIRECTOR: **MICHAEL DAHL**

ART DIRECTOR: **BOB LENTZ**

CREATIVE DIRECTOR: **HEATHER KINDSETH**

PRODUCTION SPECIALIST: **MICHELLE BIEDSCHEID**

Graphic Sparks are published by Stone Arch Books, a Capstone Imprint, 151 Good Counsel Drive, P.O. Box 669 Mankato, Minnesota 56002 www.capstonepub.com Copyright © 2011 by Stone Arch Books All rights reserved. No part of this publication may be reproduced in whole or in part, or stored in a retrieval system, or transmitted in any form or by any means, electronic, mechanical, photocopying, recording, or otherwise, without written permission of the publisher.

Library of Congress Cataloging-in-Publication Data is available on the Library of Congress website.
Library Binding: 978-1-4342-1977-0
Paperback: 978-1-4342-2804-8

Summary: With the evil Echo around, Halo Nightly faces her strongest villain yet — herself. When Echo steals Halo's candy, Halo is forced to battle someone who is every bit as powerful as she is.

Printed in the United States of America in Stevens Point, Wisconsin.
032010
005741WZF10

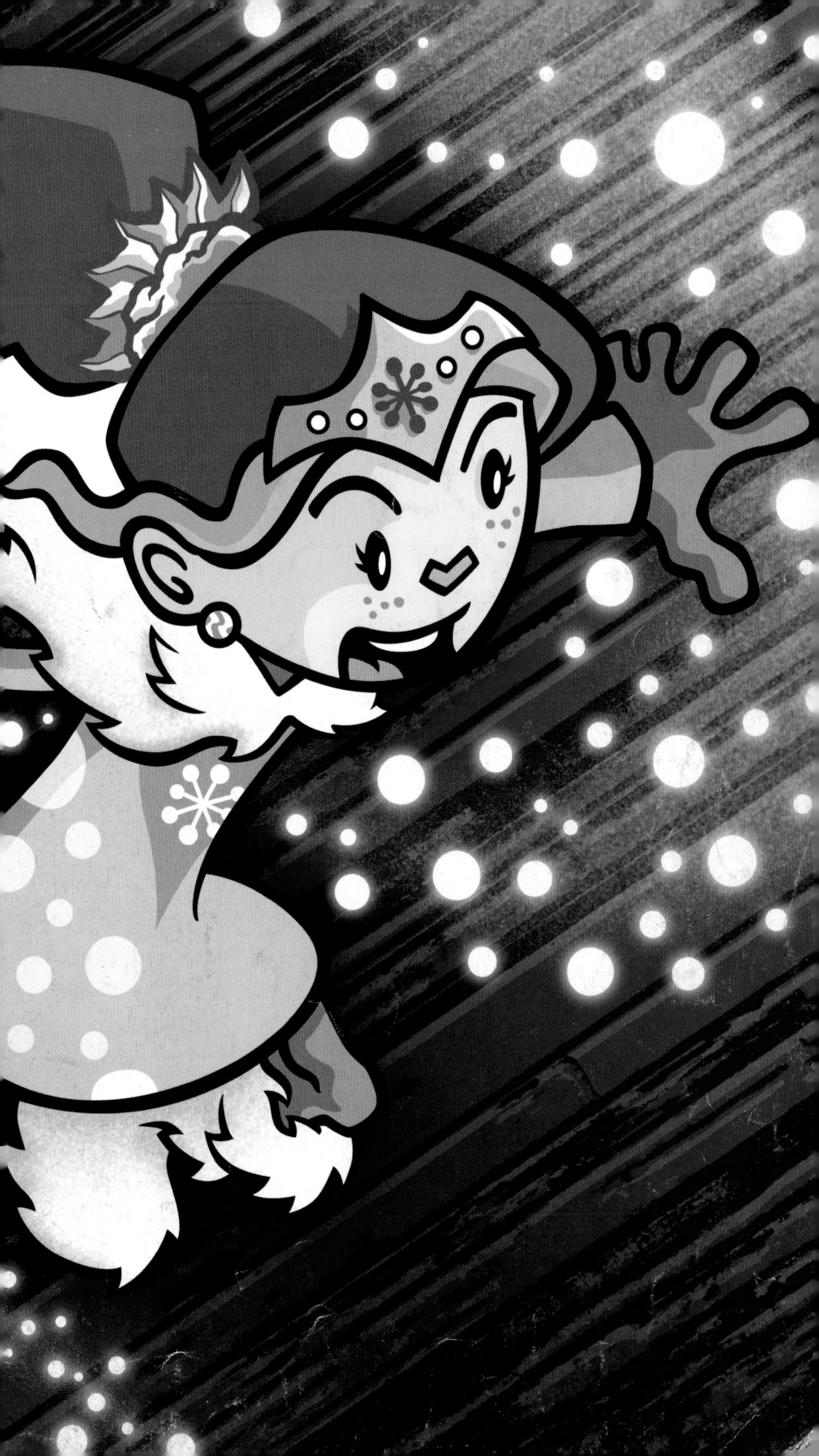

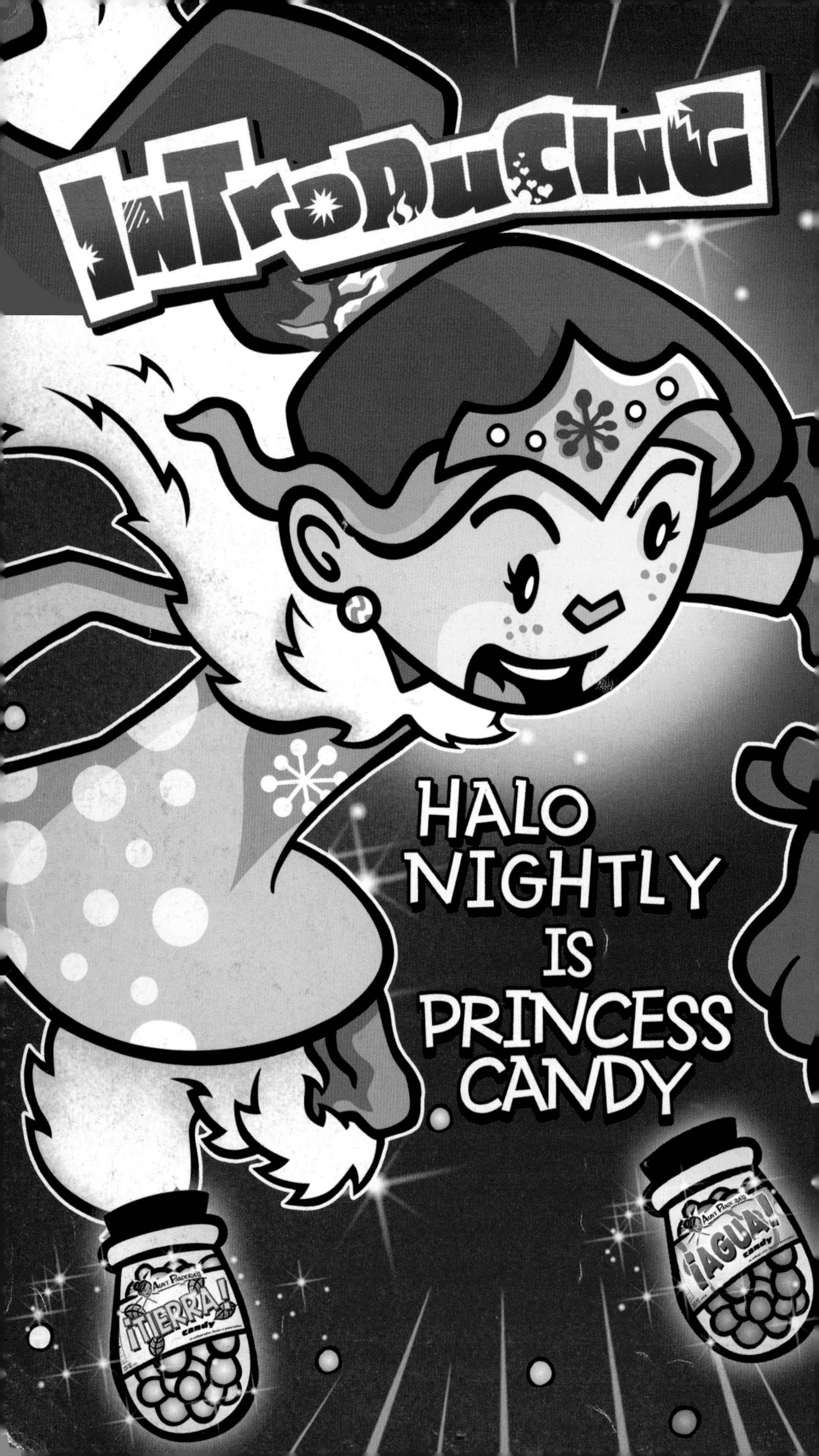
INTRODUCING
HALO NIGHTLY IS PRINCESS CANDY
AUNT PANDORA'S
¡TIERRA!
candy
AUNT PANDORA'S
¡AGUA!
candy

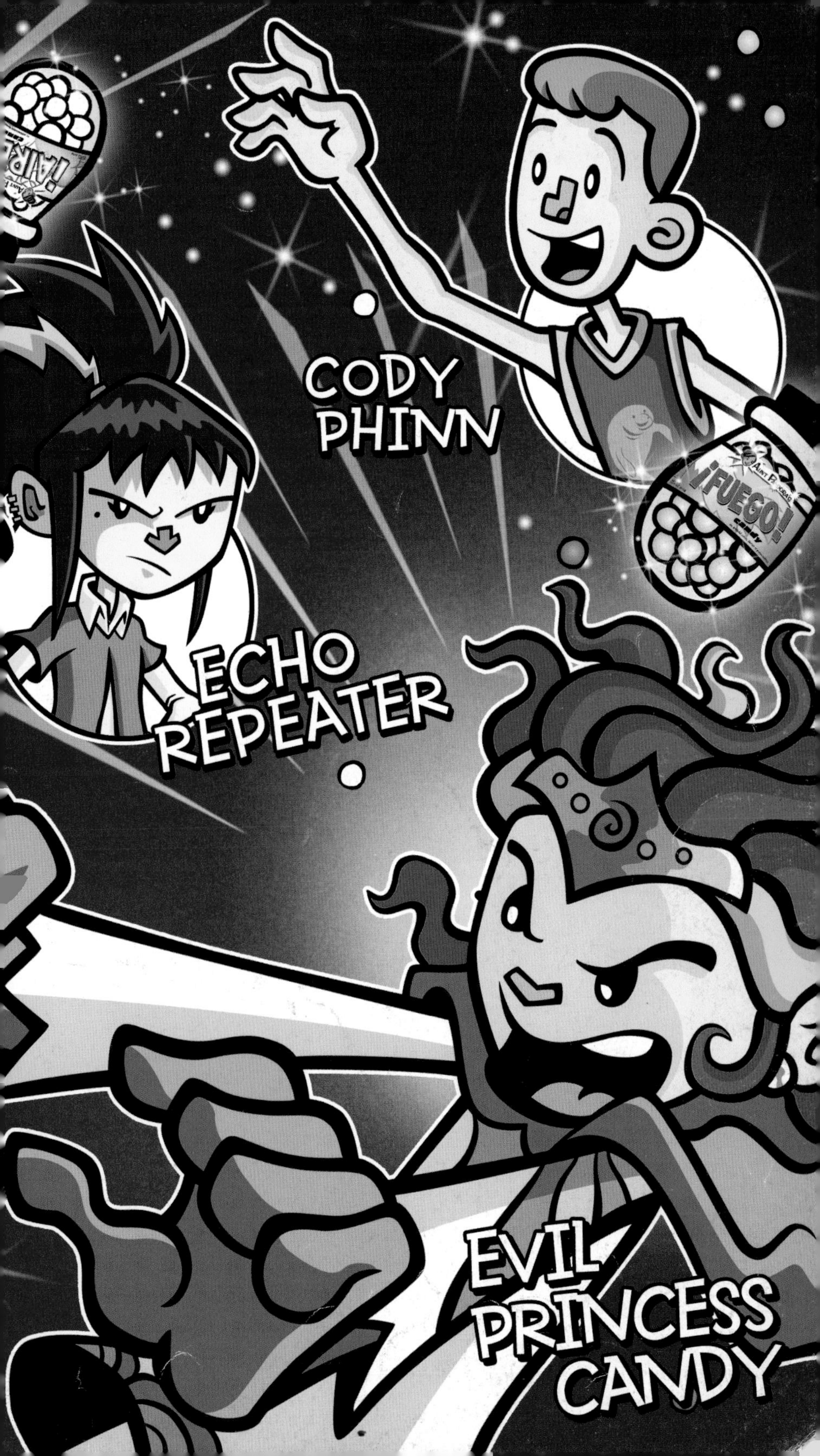
CODY PHINN
ECHO REPEATER
EVIL PRINCESS CANDY
¡FUEGO!

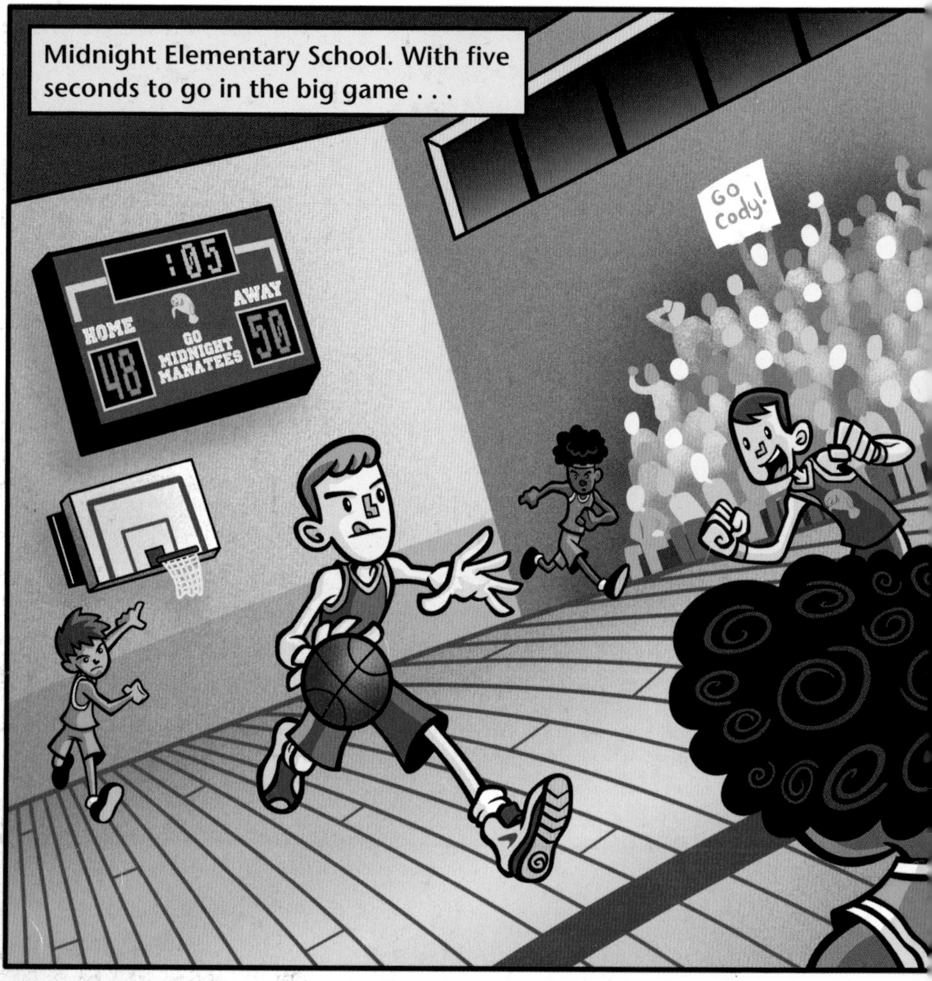
Midnight Elementary School. With five seconds to go in the big game . . .
:05
HOME
48
AWAY
50
GO MIDNIGHT MANATEES
Go cody!

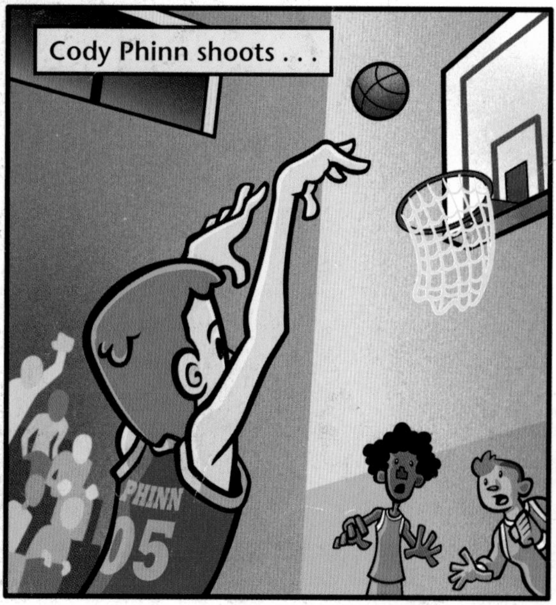
Cody Phinn shoots . . .
PHINN
05

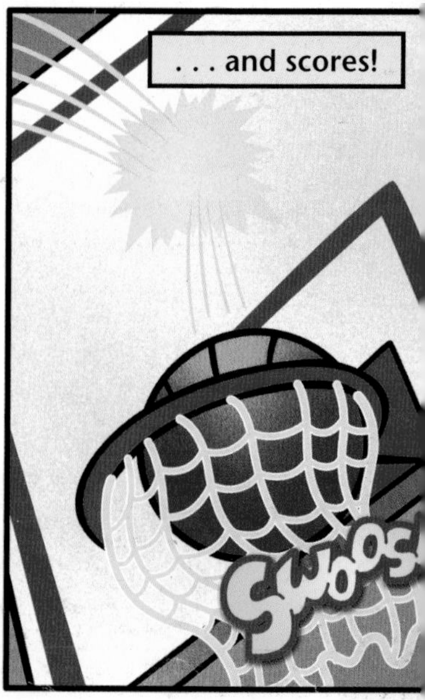
. . . and scores!

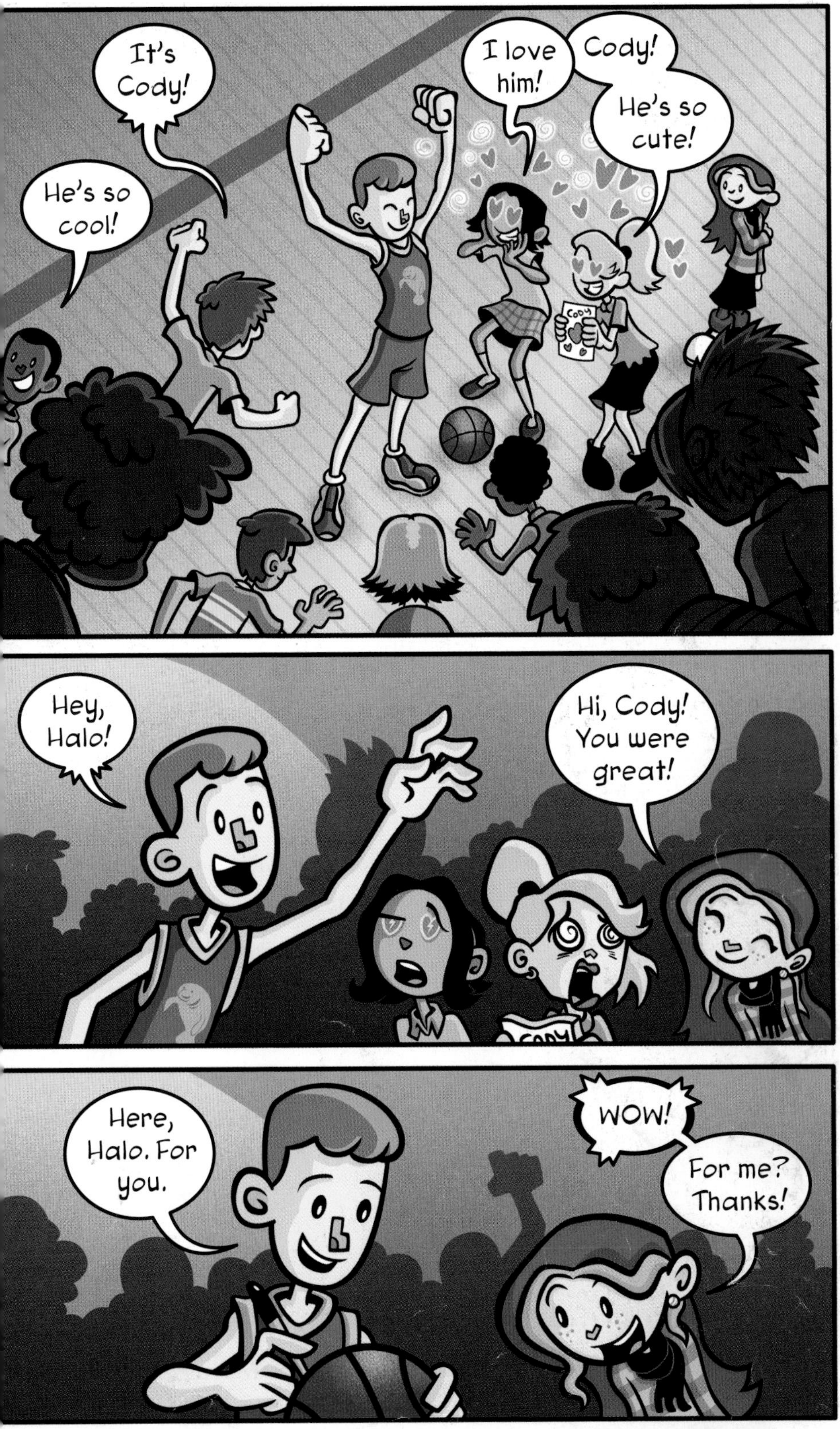
It's Cody!
He's so cool!
I love him!
Cody!
He's so cute!
Hey, Halo!
Hi, Cody! You were great!
Here, Halo. For you.
WOW!
For me? Thanks!

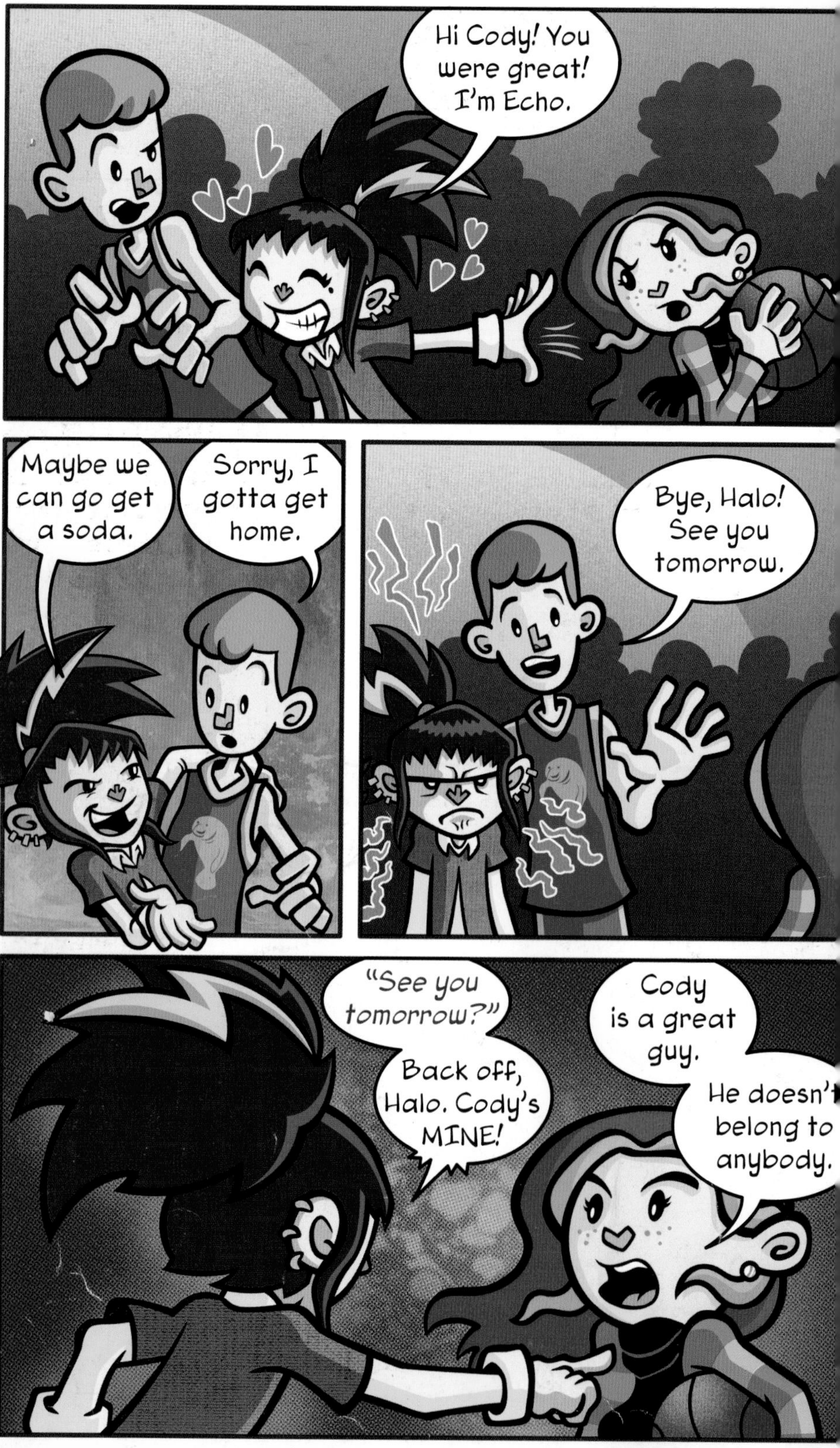
Hi Cody! You were great! I'm Echo.
Maybe we can go get a soda.
Sorry, I gotta get home.
Bye, Halo! See you tomorrow.
"See you tomorrow?"
Back off, Halo. Cody's MINE!
Cody is a great guy.
He doesn't belong to anybody.

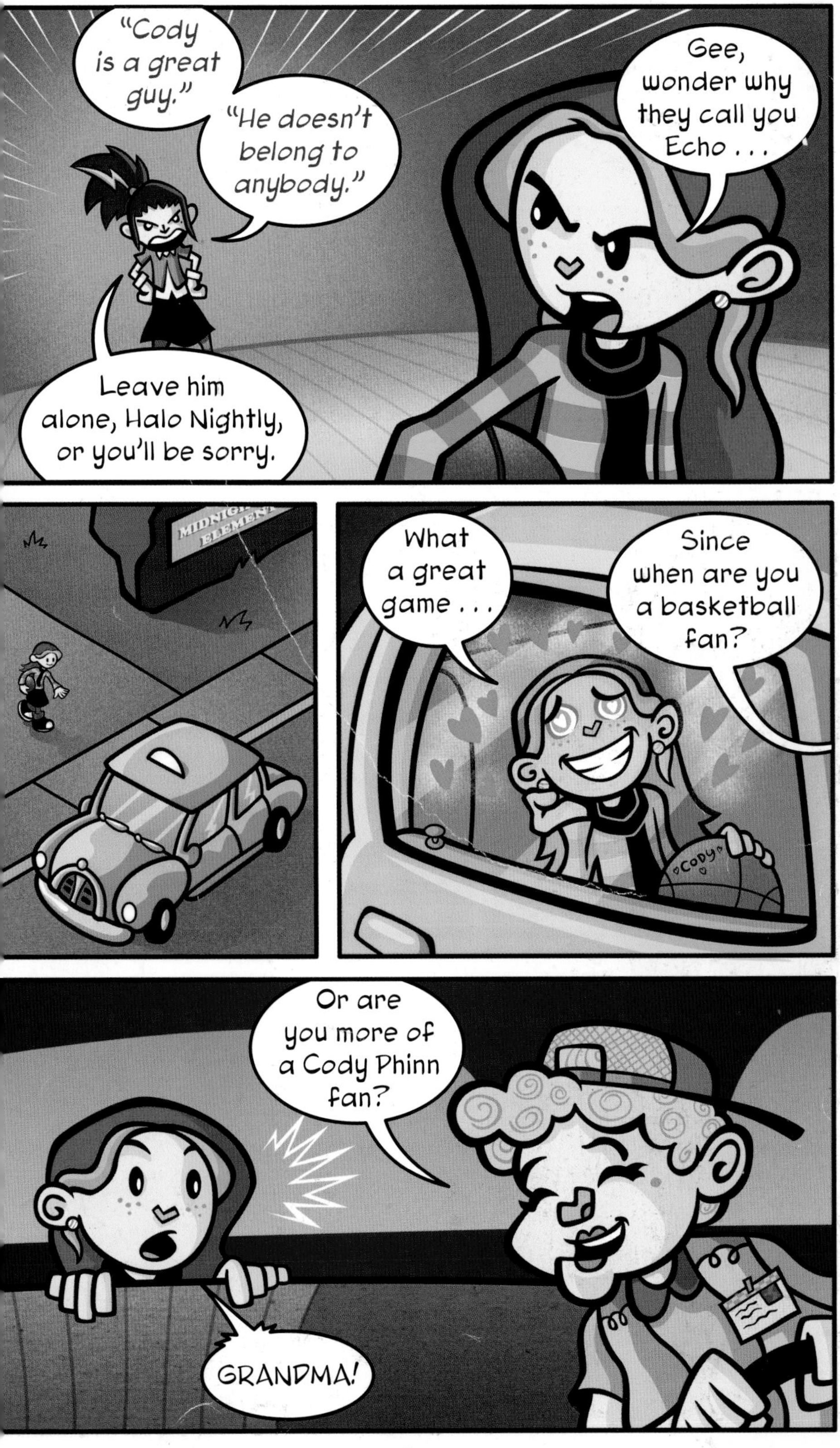
"Cody is a great guy."
"He doesn't belong to anybody."
Gee, wonder why they call you Echo . . .
Leave him alone, Halo Nightly, or you'll be sorry.
MIDNIGHT ELEMENT
What a great game . . .
Since when are you a basketball fan?
CODY
Or are you more of a Cody Phinn fan?
GRANDMA!

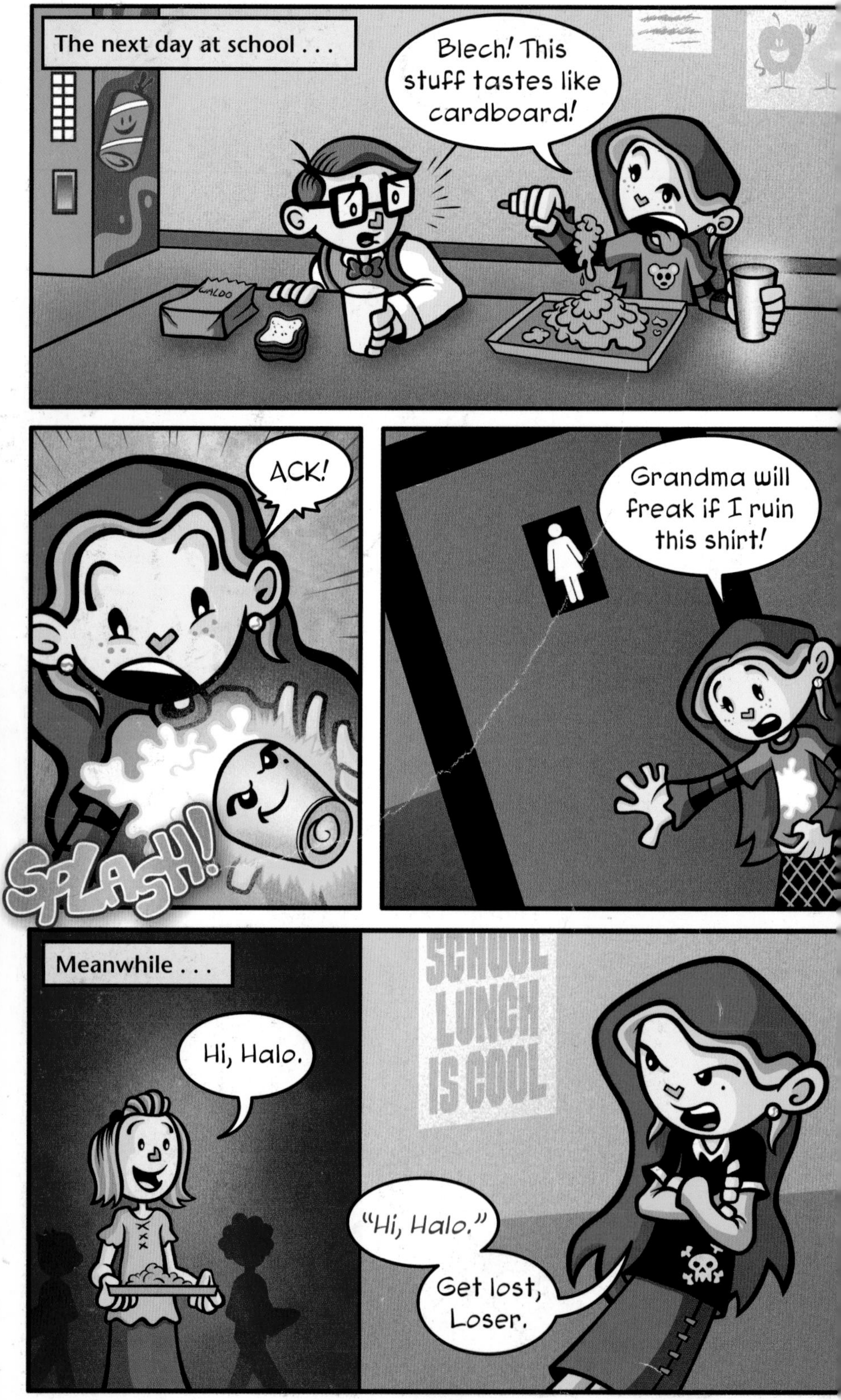
The next day at school . . .
Blech! This stuff tastes like cardboard!
ACK!
SPLASH!
Grandma will freak if I ruin this shirt!
Meanwhile . . .
SCHOOL LUNCH IS COOL
Hi, Halo.
"Hi, Halo."
Get lost, Loser.

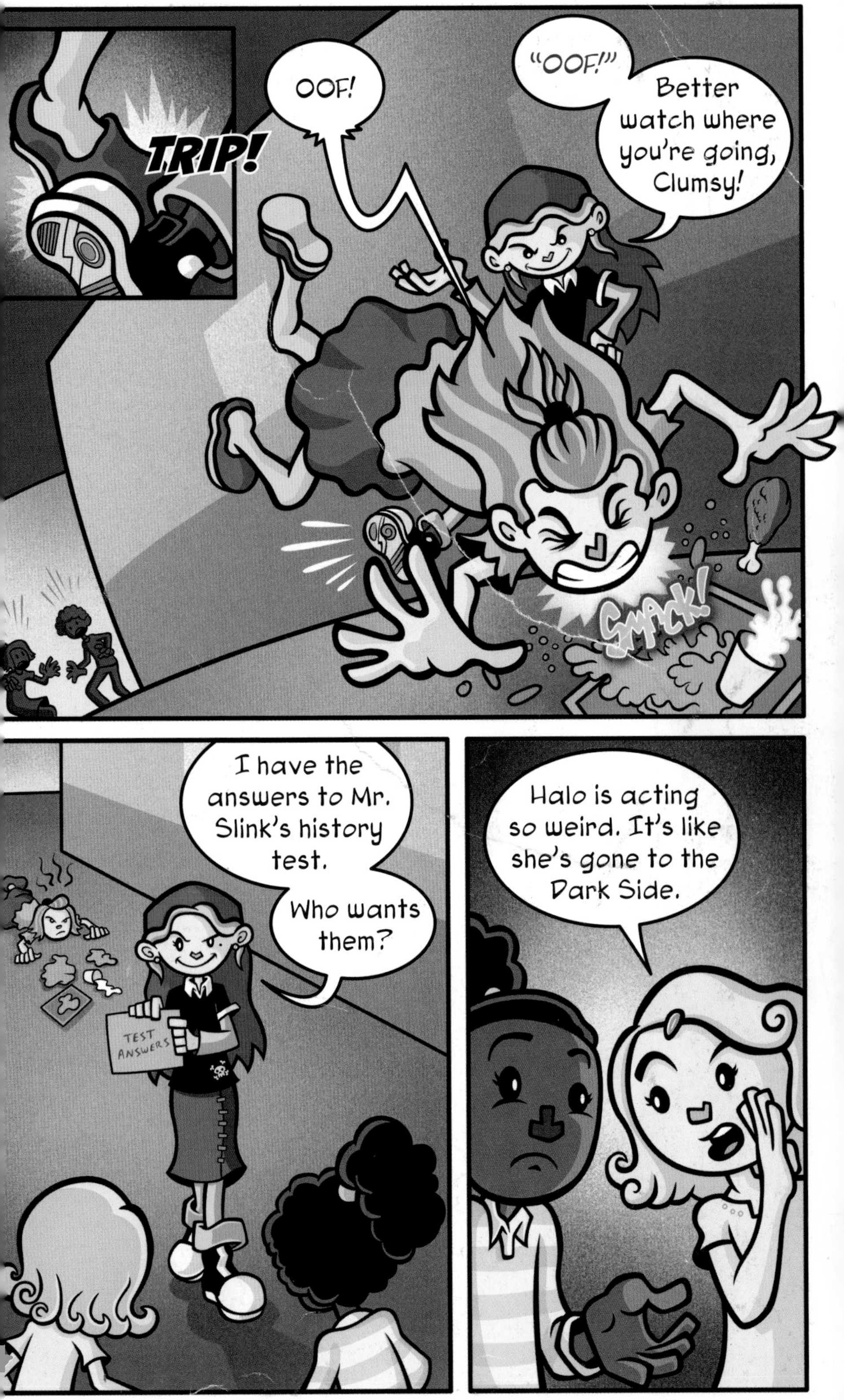
TRIP!
OOF!
"OOF!"
Better watch where you're going, Clumsy!
SMACK!
I have the answers to Mr. Slink's history test.
Who wants them?
TEST ANSWERS
Halo is acting so weird. It's like she's gone to the Dark Side.

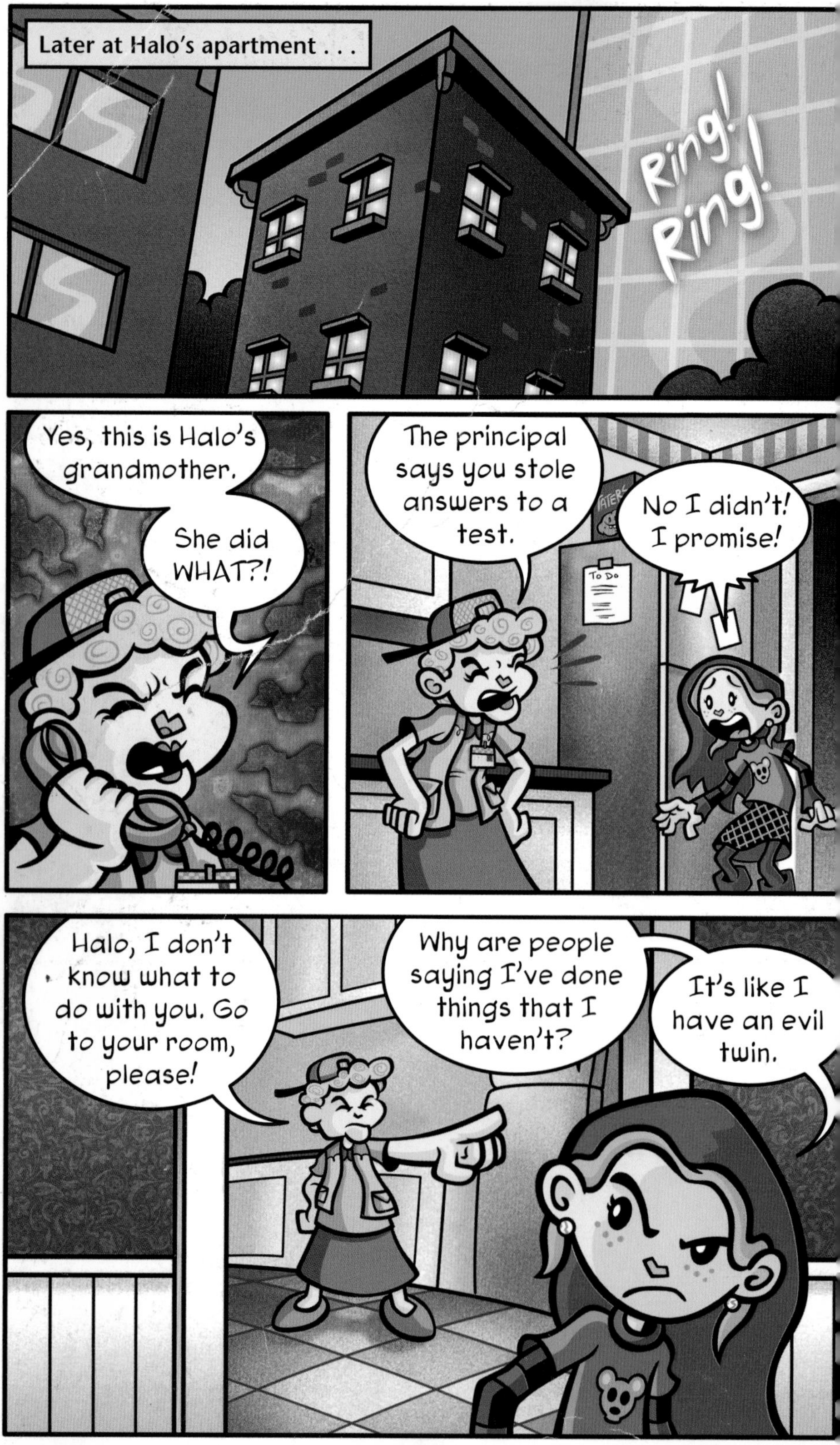
Later at Halo's apartment . . .
Ring! Ring!
Yes, this is Halo's grandmother.
She did WHAT?!
The principal says you stole answers to a test.
No I didn't! I promise!
To Do
Halo, I don't know what to do with you. Go to your room, please!
Why are people saying I've done things that I haven't?
It's like I have an evil twin.

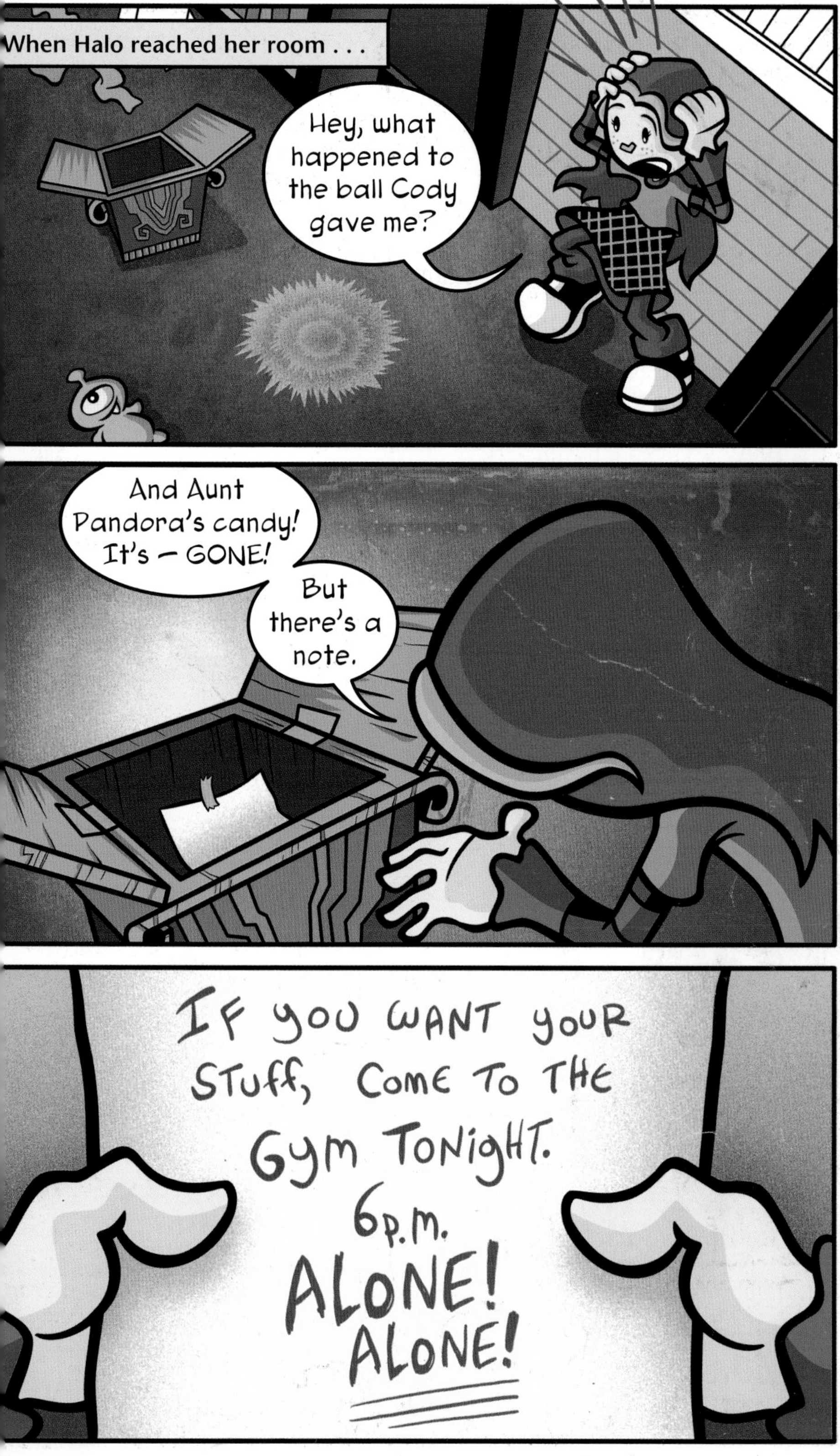
When Halo reached her room . . .
Hey, what happened to the ball Cody gave me?
And Aunt Pandora's candy! It's — GONE!
But there's a note.
IF YOU WANT YOUR STUFF, COME TO THE GYM TONIGHT. 6 P.M. ALONE! ALONE!

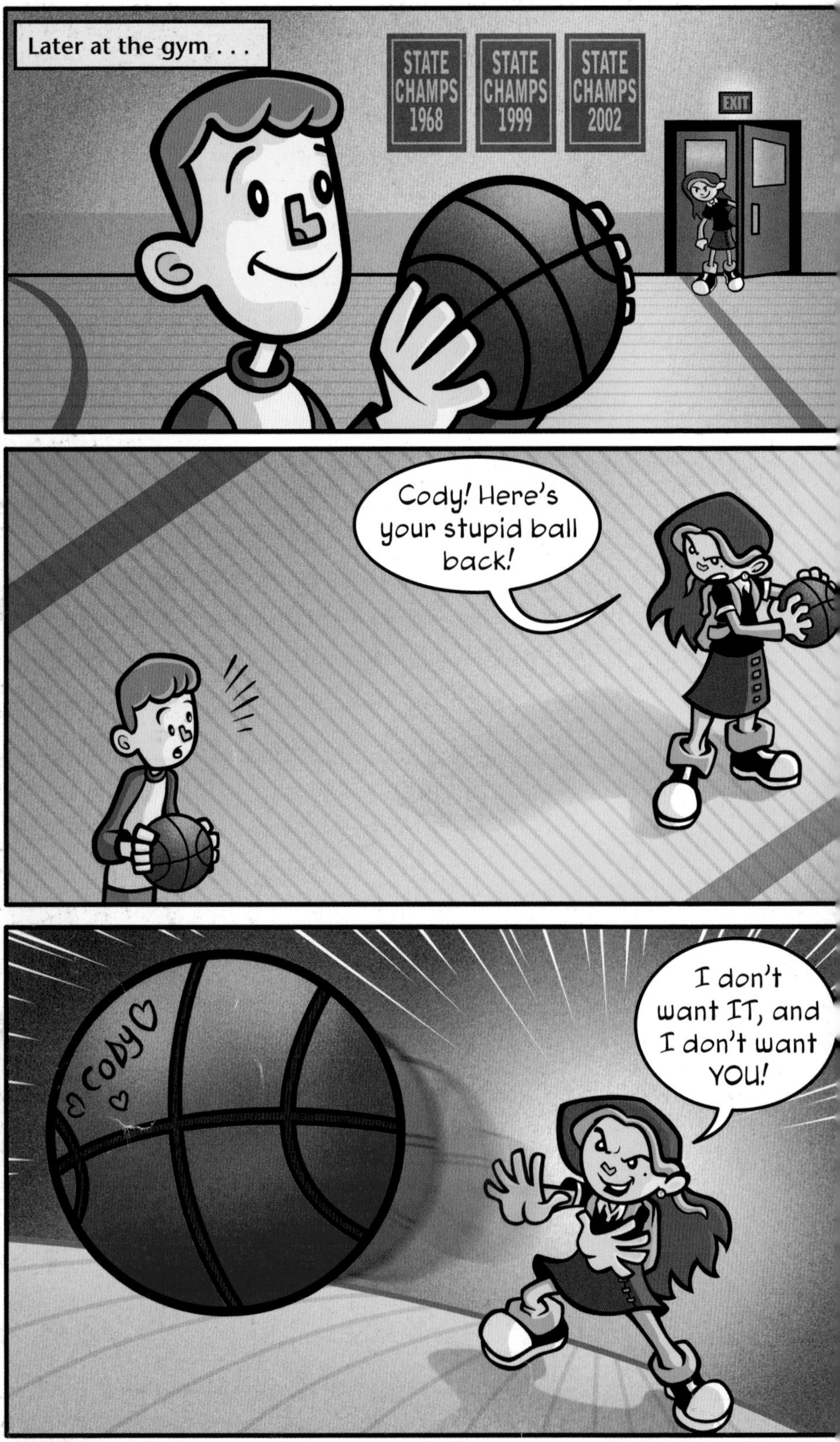
Later at the gym . . .
STATE CHAMPS 1968
STATE CHAMPS 1999
STATE CHAMPS 2002
EXIT
Cody! Here's your stupid ball back!
Cody
I don't want IT, and I don't want YOU!

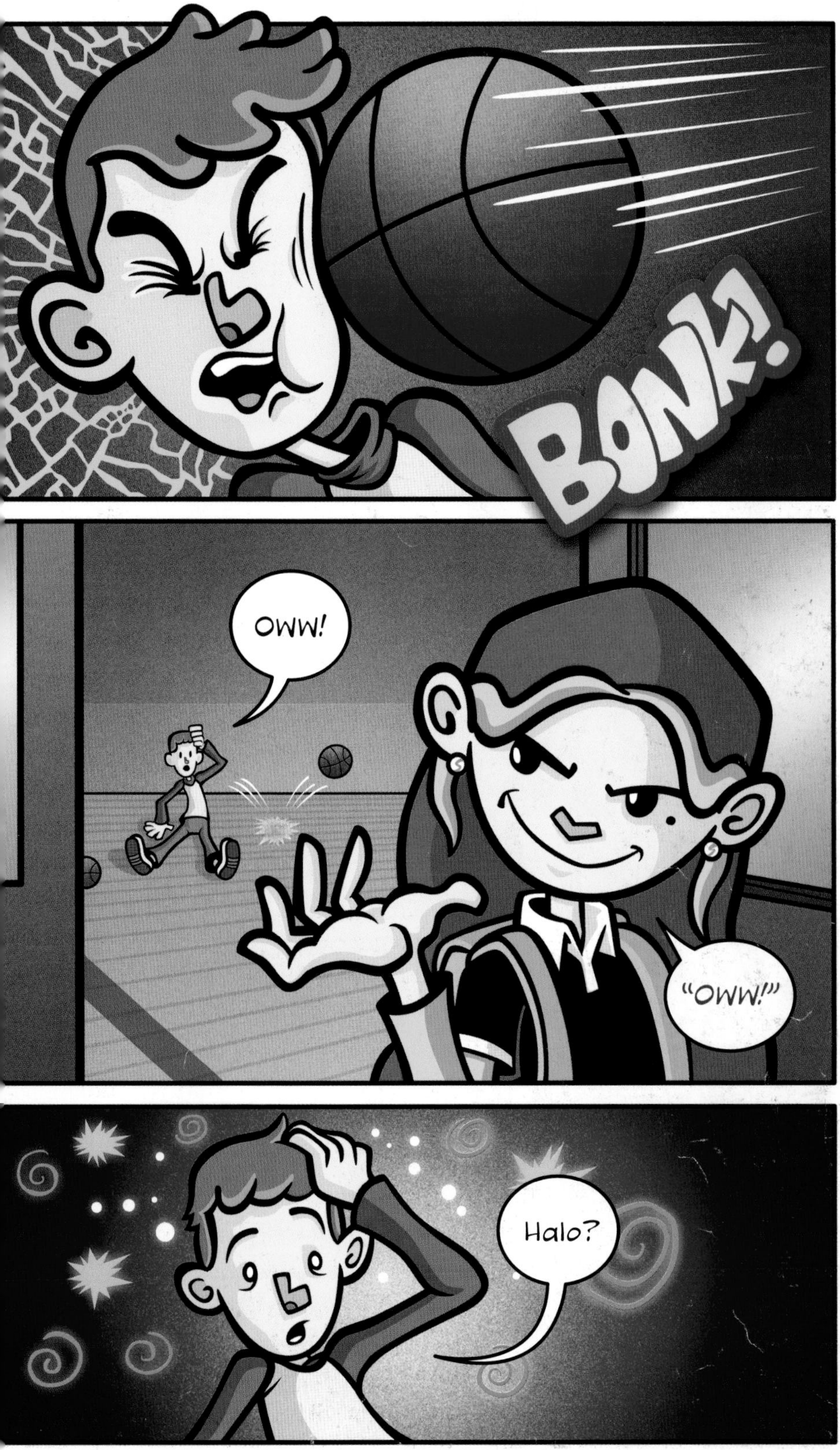
BONK!
OWW!
"OWW!"
Halo?

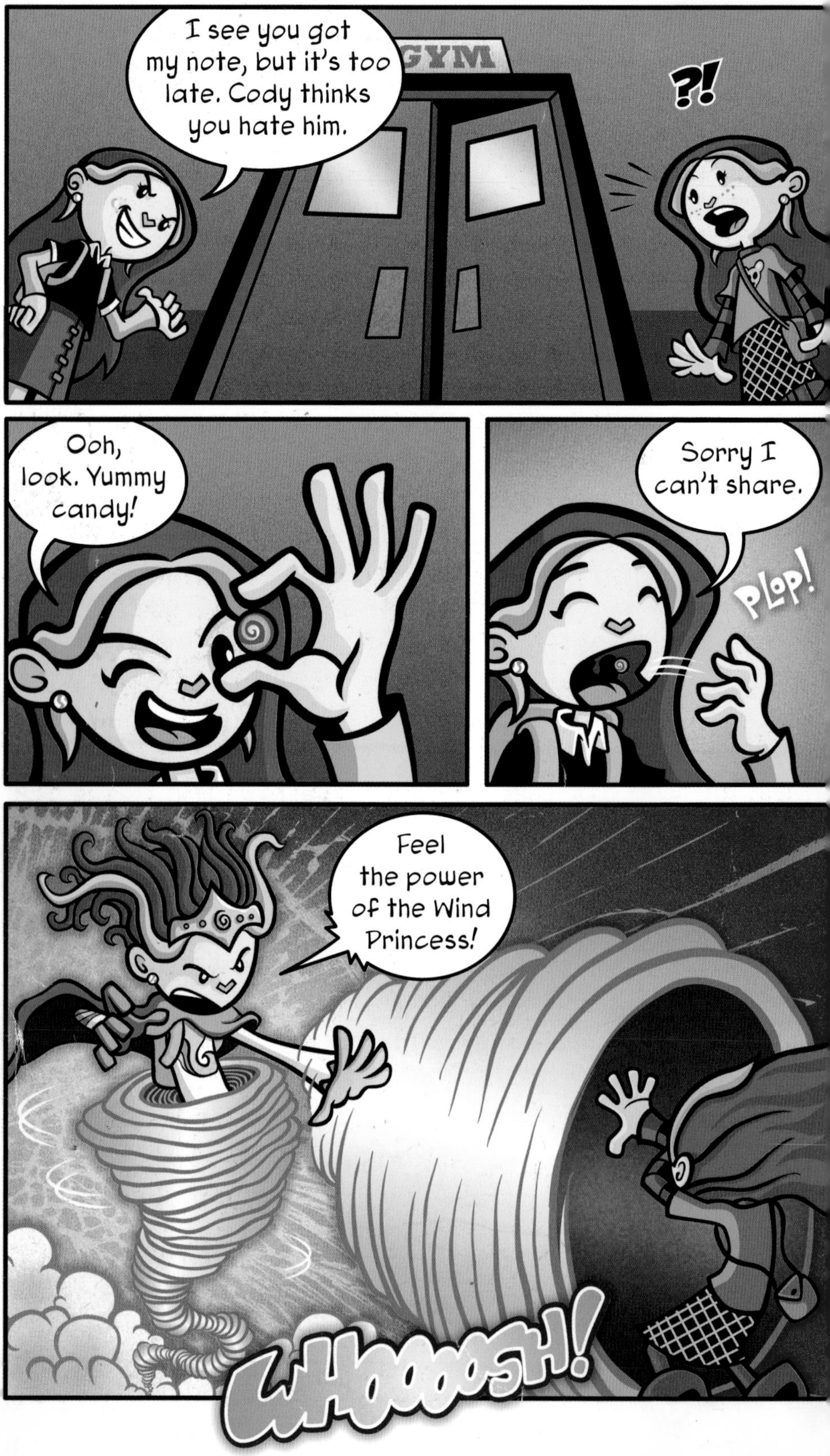
GYM
I see you got my note, but it's too late. Cody thinks you hate him.
?!
Ooh, look. Yummy candy!
Sorry I can't share.
PLOP!
Feel the power of the Wind Princess!
WHOOOOSH!

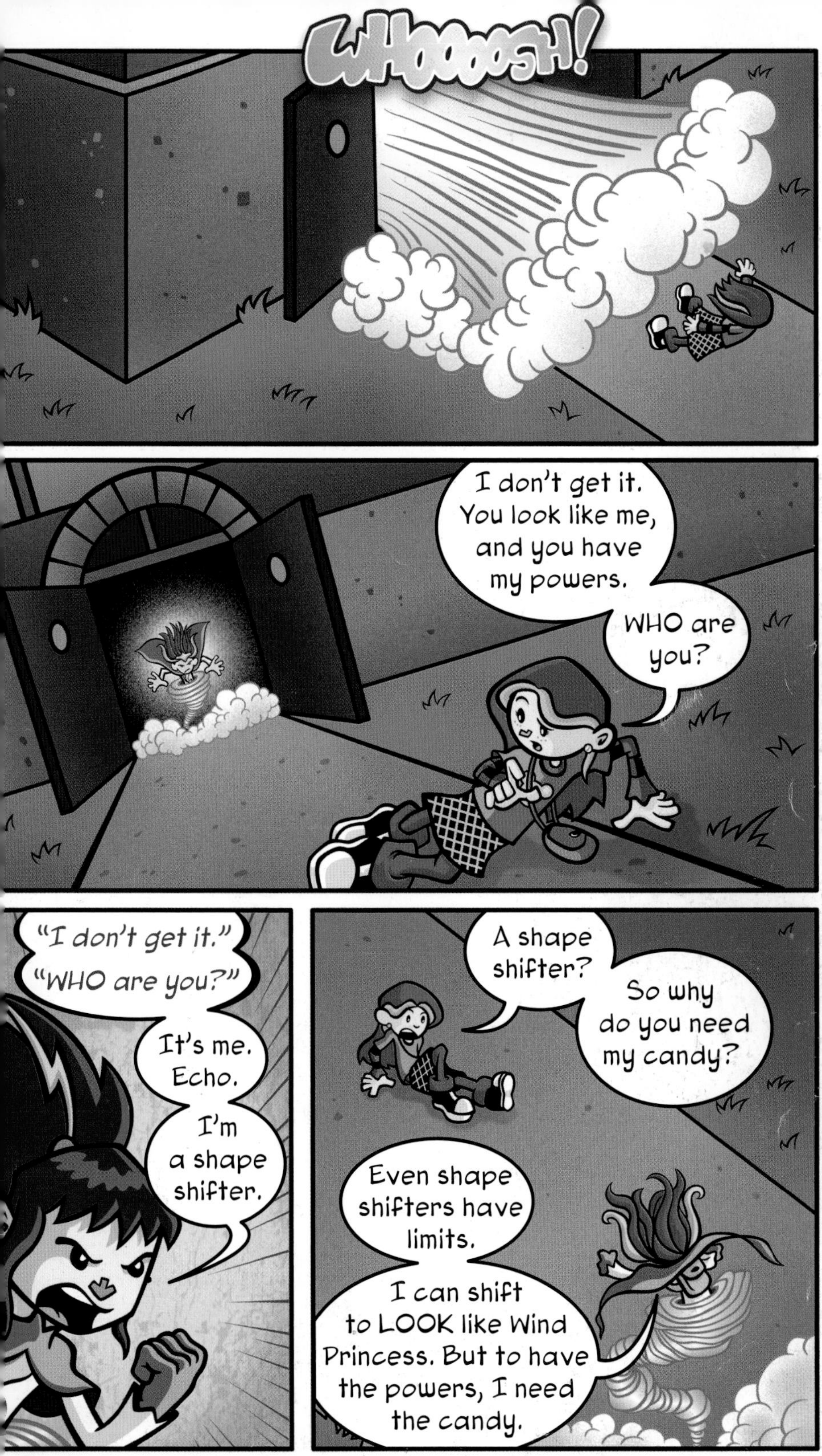
WHOOOOSH!
I don't get it. You look like me, and you have my powers.
WHO are you?
"I don't get it."
"WHO are you?"
It's me. Echo.
I'm a shape shifter.
A shape shifter?
So why do you need my candy?
Even shape shifters have limits.
I can shift to LOOK like Wind Princess. But to have the powers, I need the candy.

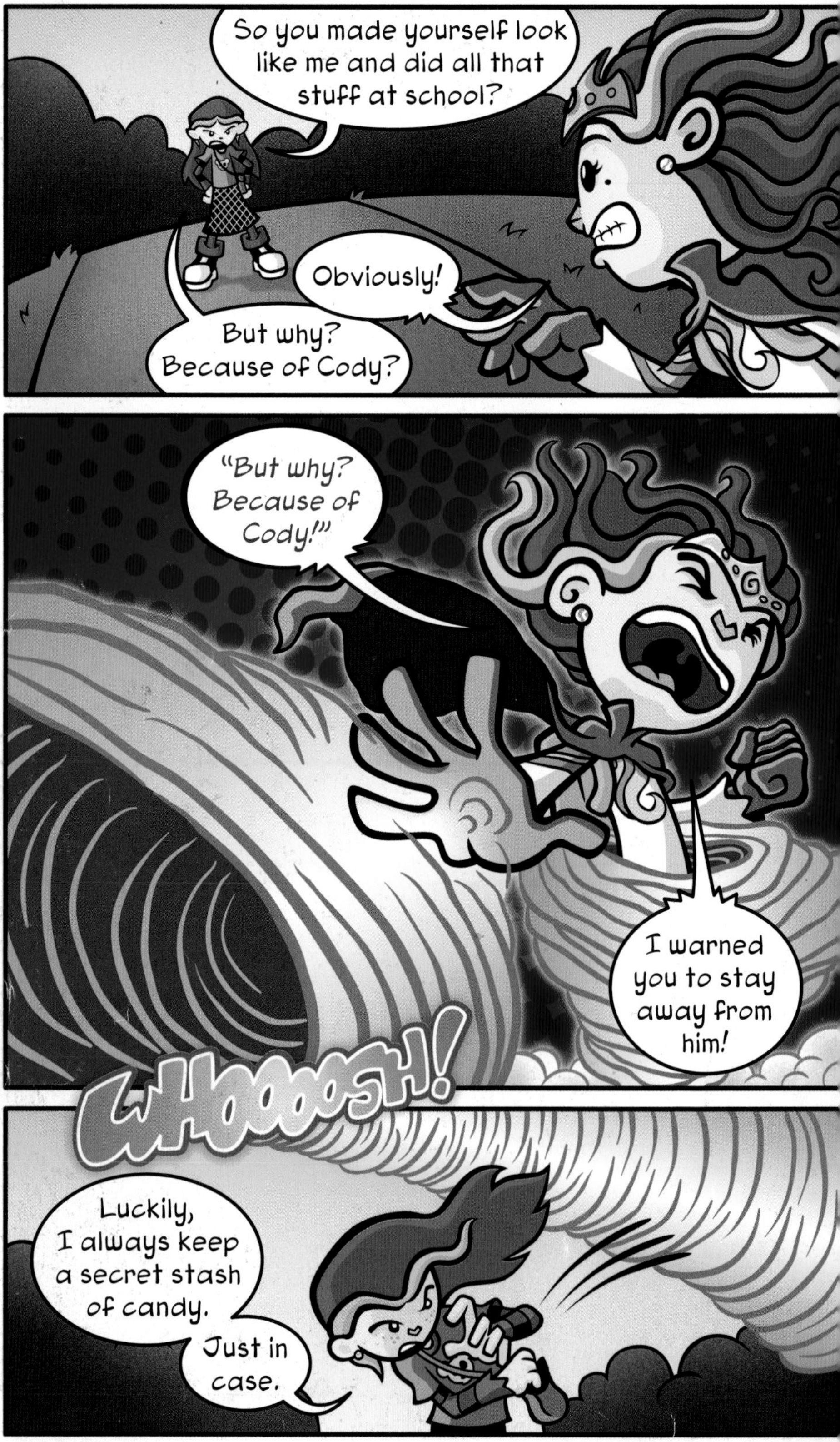

So you made yourself look like me and did all that stuff at school?
Obviously!
But why? Because of Cody?
"But why? Because of Cody!"
I warned you to stay away from him!
WHOOOOSH!
Luckily, I always keep a secret stash of candy.
Just in case.

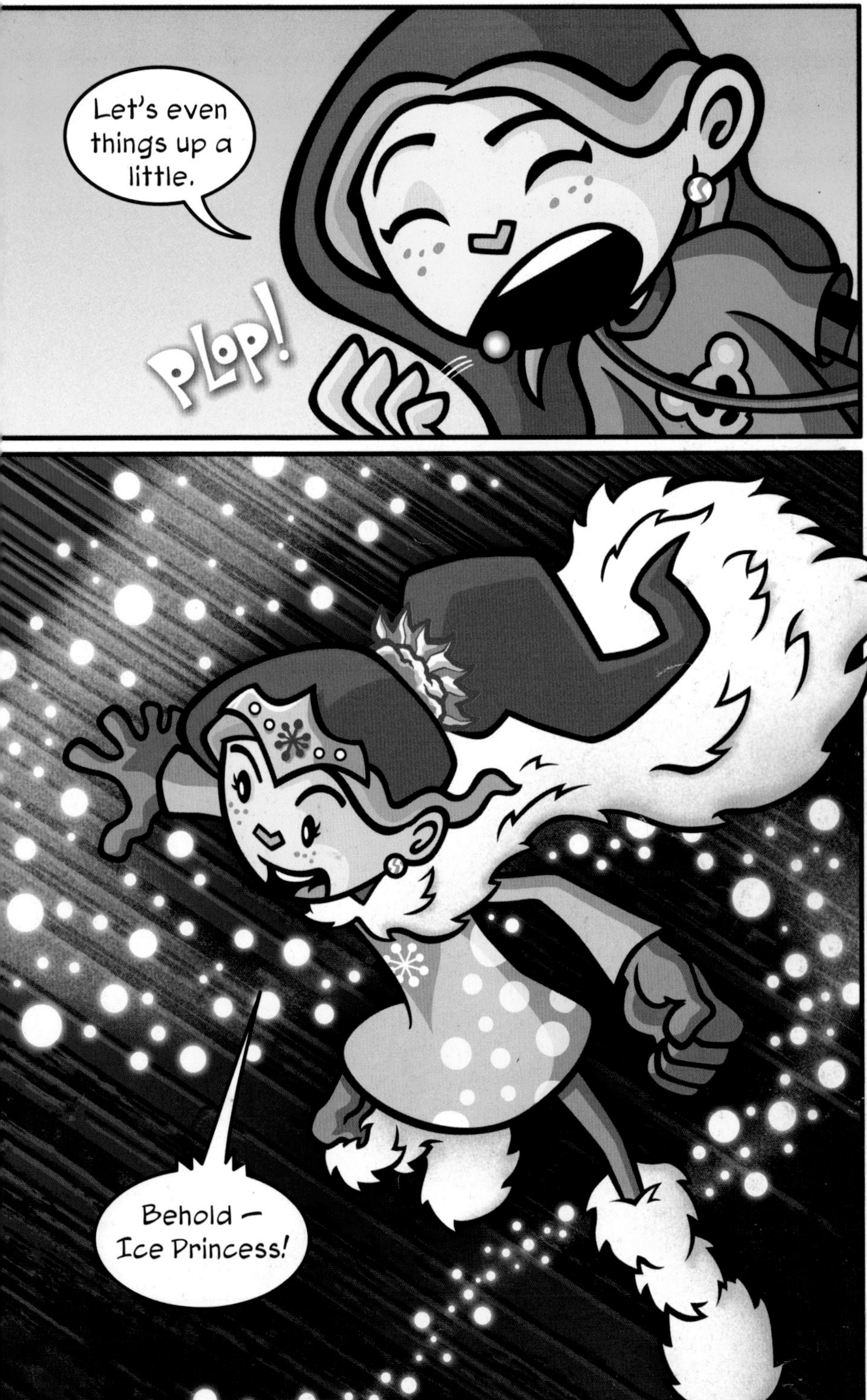
Let's even things up a little.
PLOP!
Behold — Ice Princess!

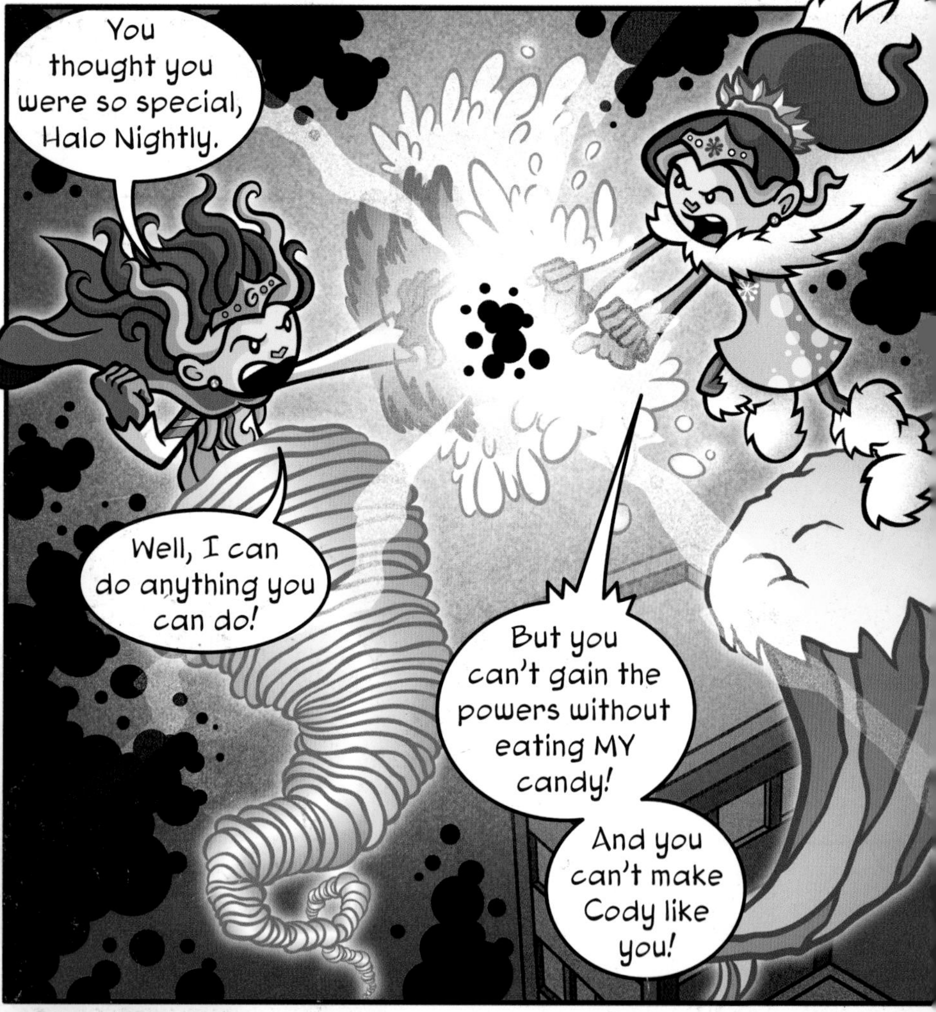
You thought you were so special, Halo Nightly.
Well, I can do anything you can do!
But you can't gain the powers without eating MY candy!
And you can't make Cody like you!

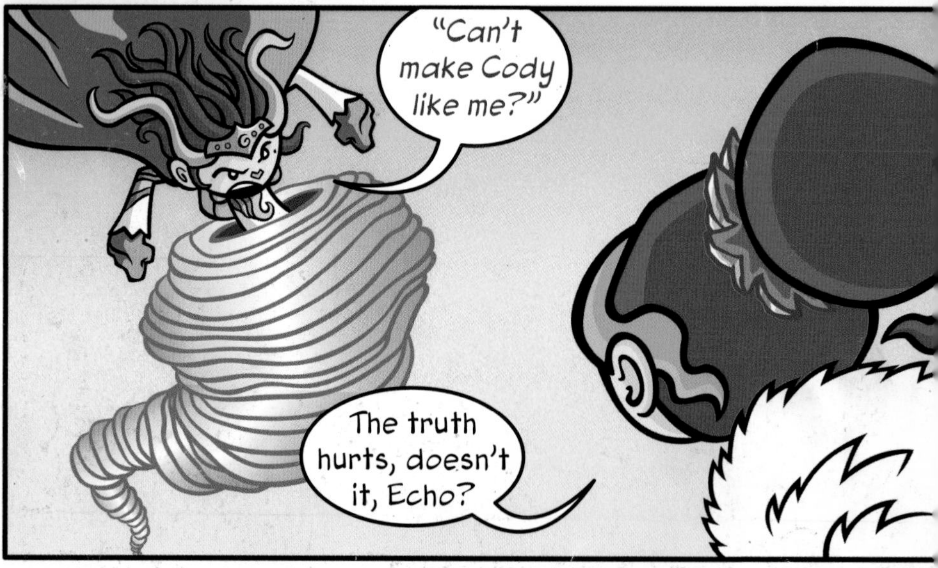
"Can't make Cody like me?"
The truth hurts, doesn't it, Echo?

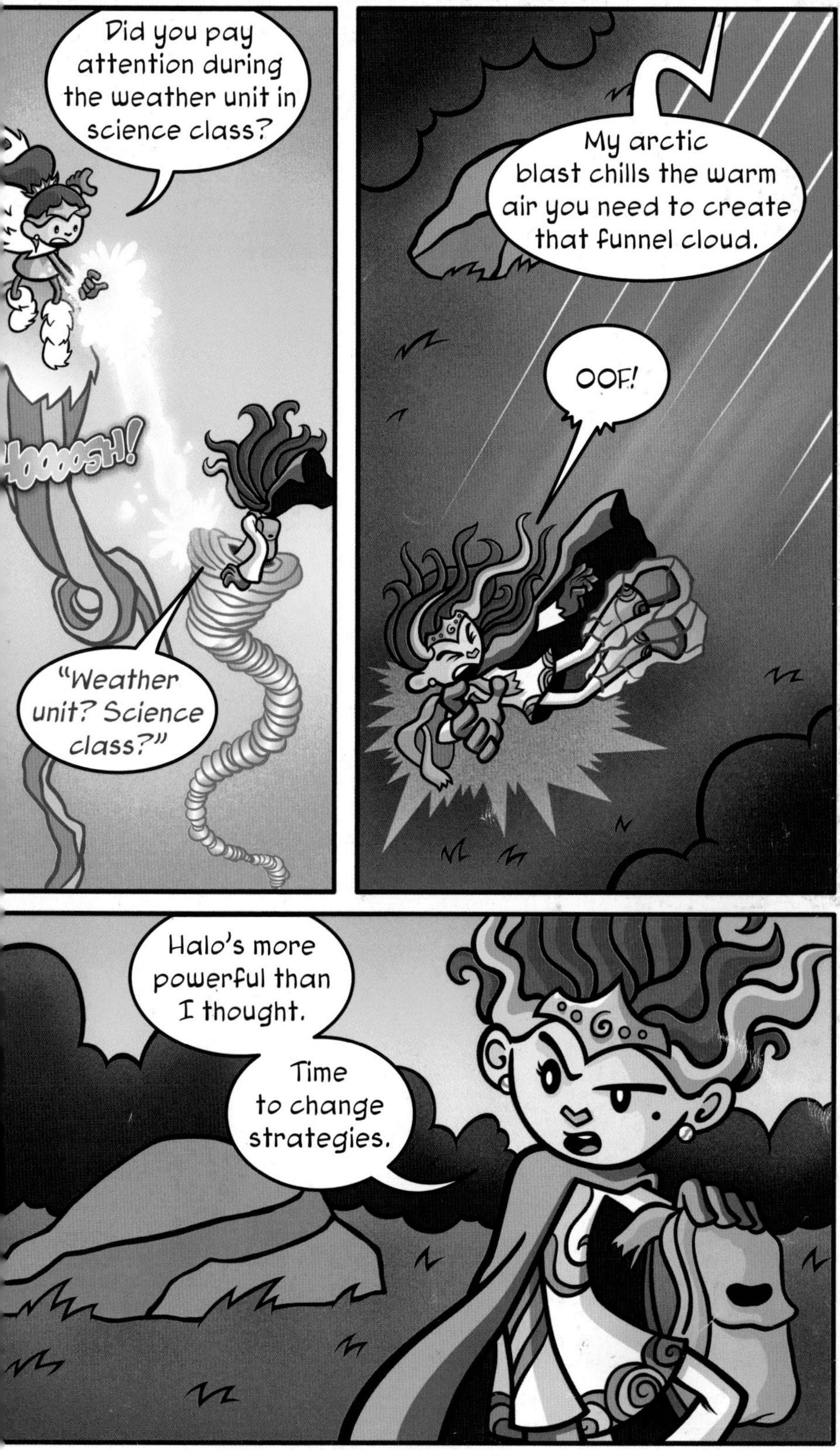
Did you pay attention during the weather unit in science class?
WHOOOOSH!
"Weather unit? Science class?"
My arctic blast chills the warm air you need to create that funnel cloud.
OOF!
Halo's more powerful than I thought.
Time to change strategies.

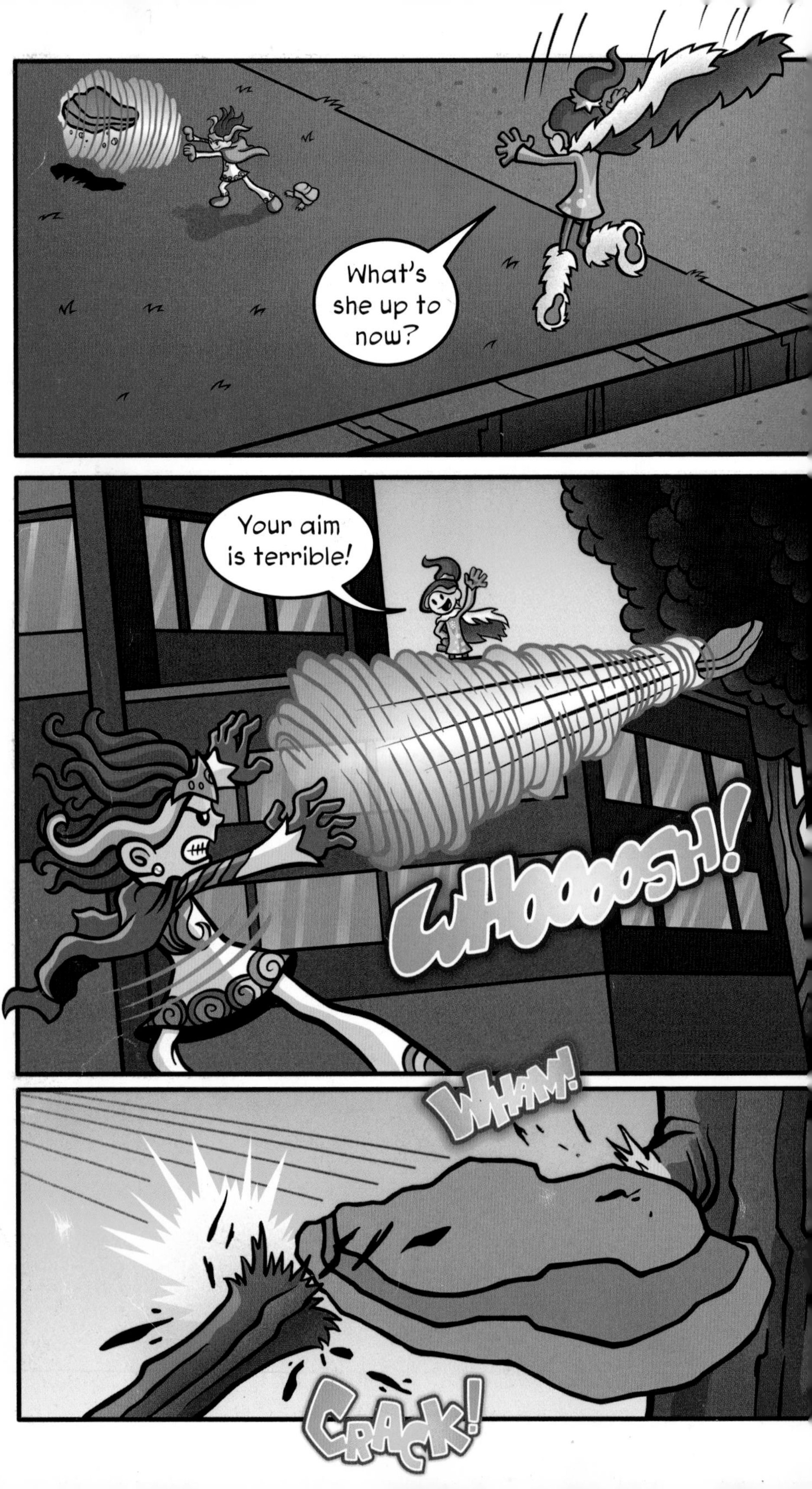
What's she up to now?
Your aim is terrible!
WHOOOOSH!
WHAM!
CRACK!

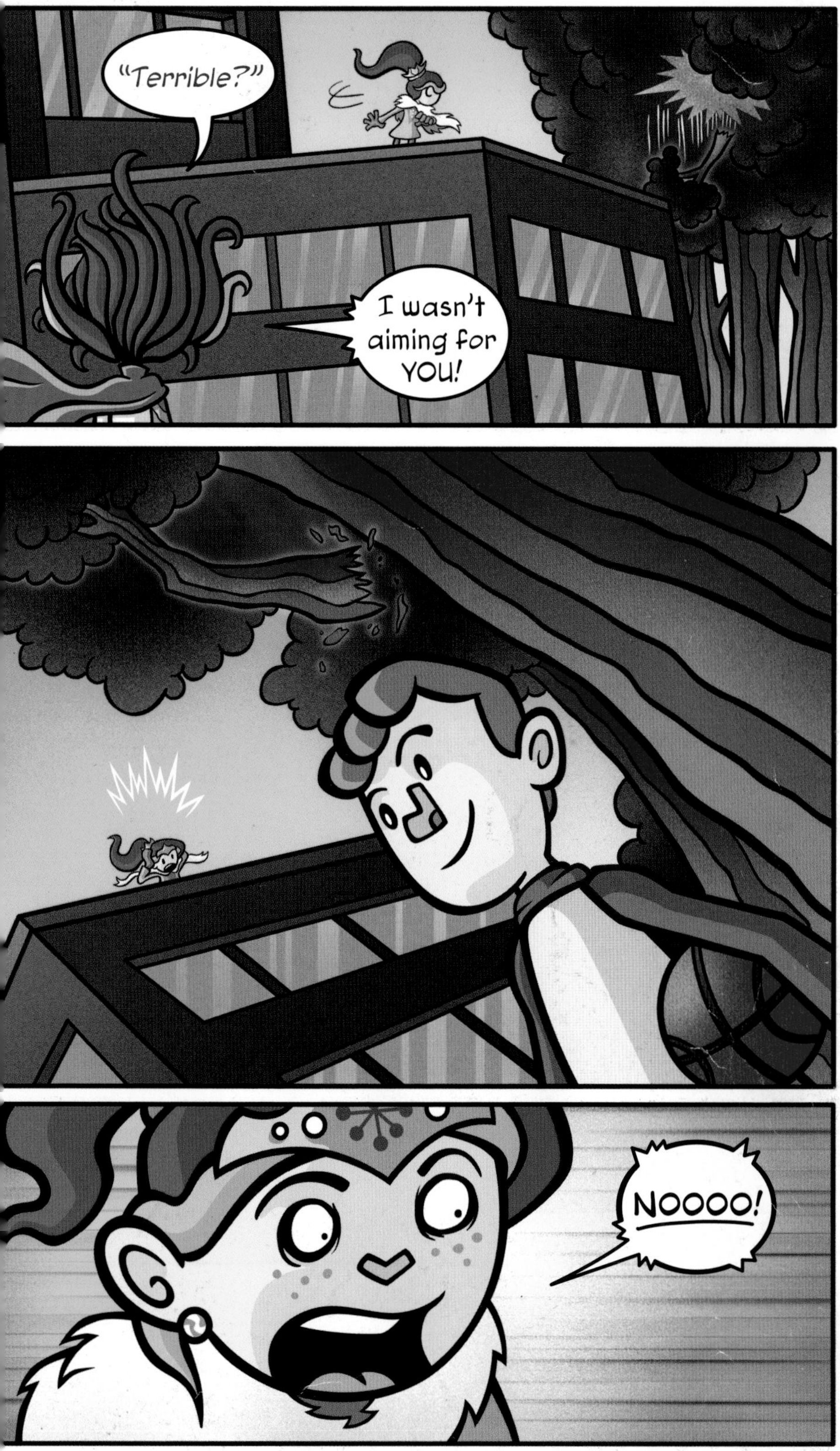
"Terrible?"
I wasn't aiming for YOU!
NOOOO!

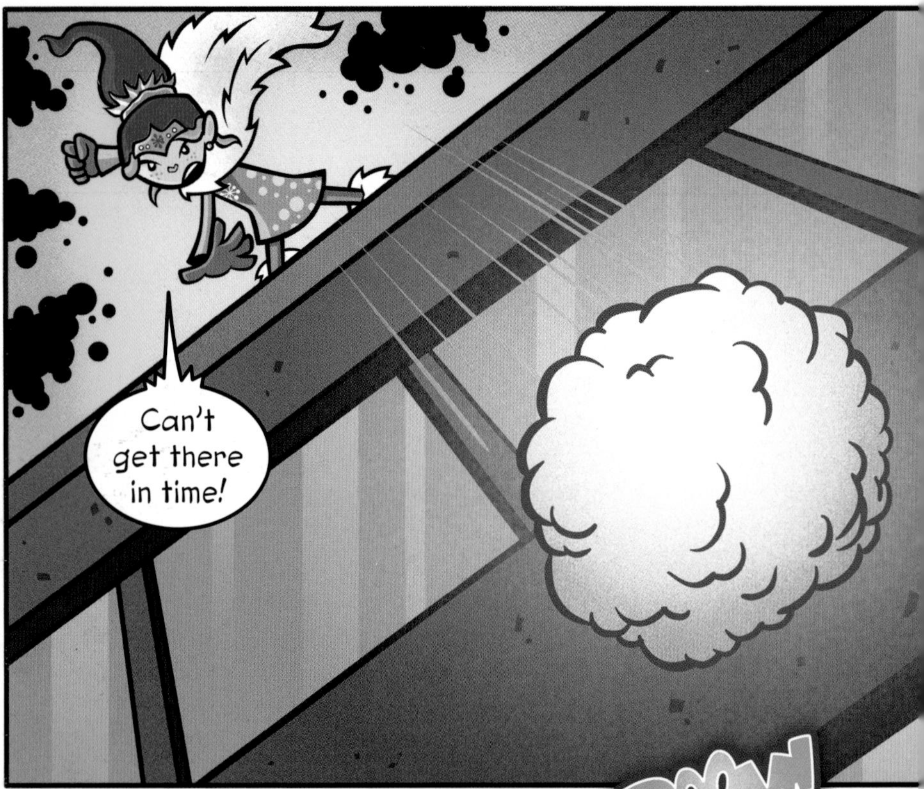
Can't get there in time!

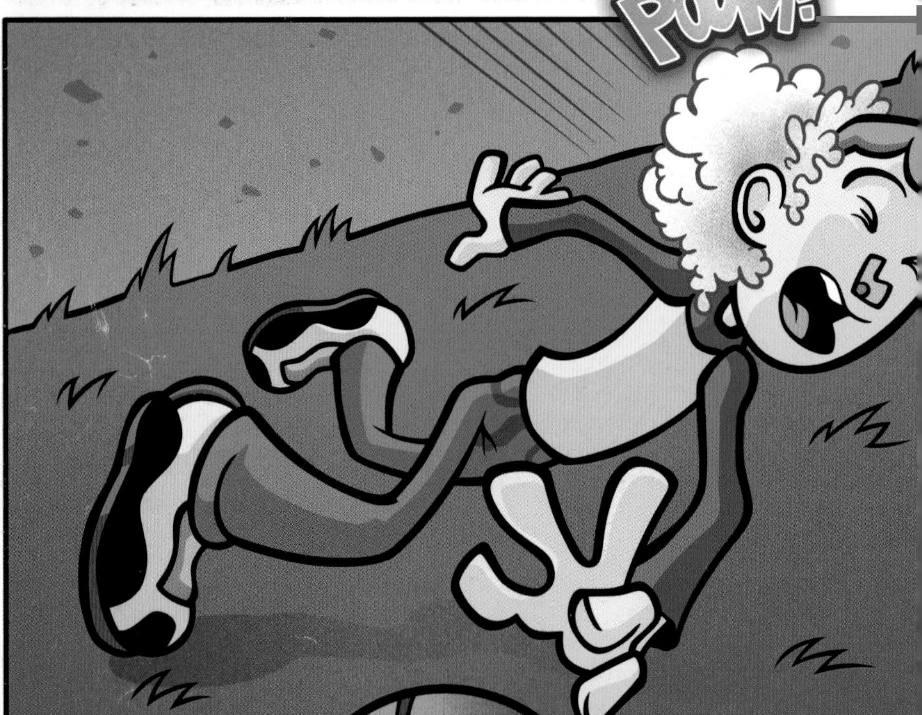
POOM!

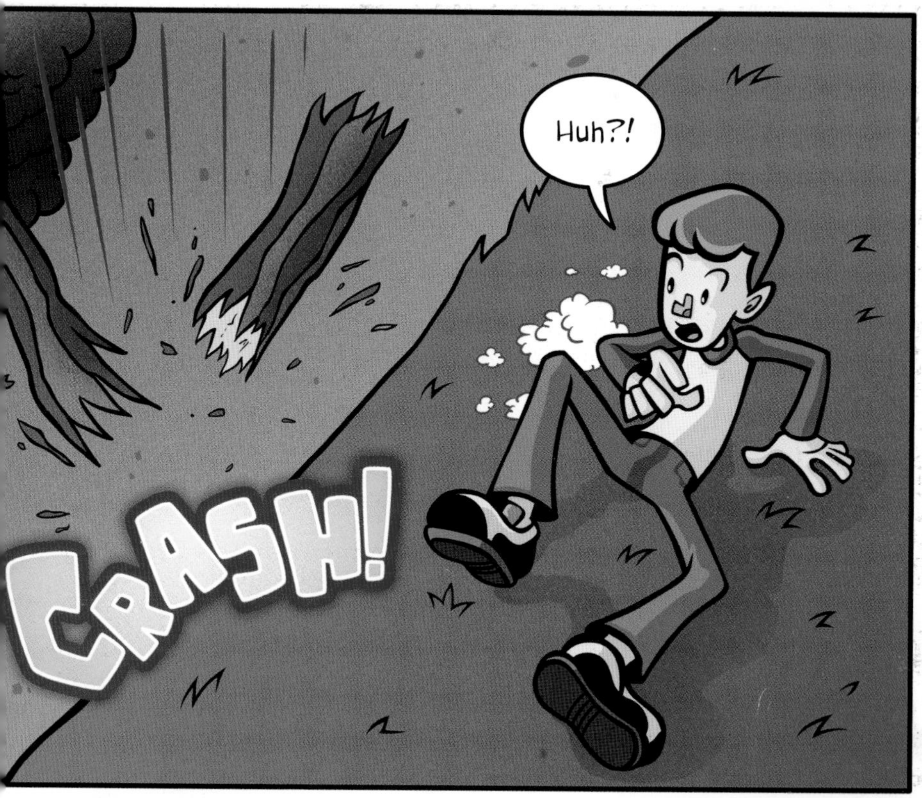
CRASH!
Huh?!

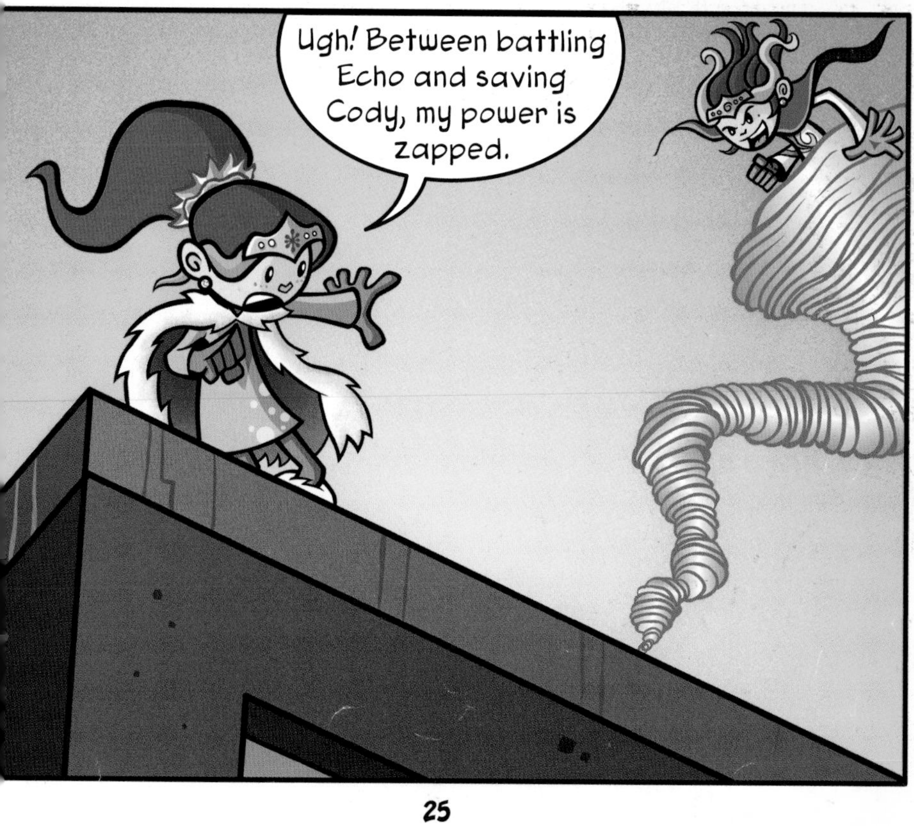
Ugh! Between battling Echo and saving Cody, my power is zapped.

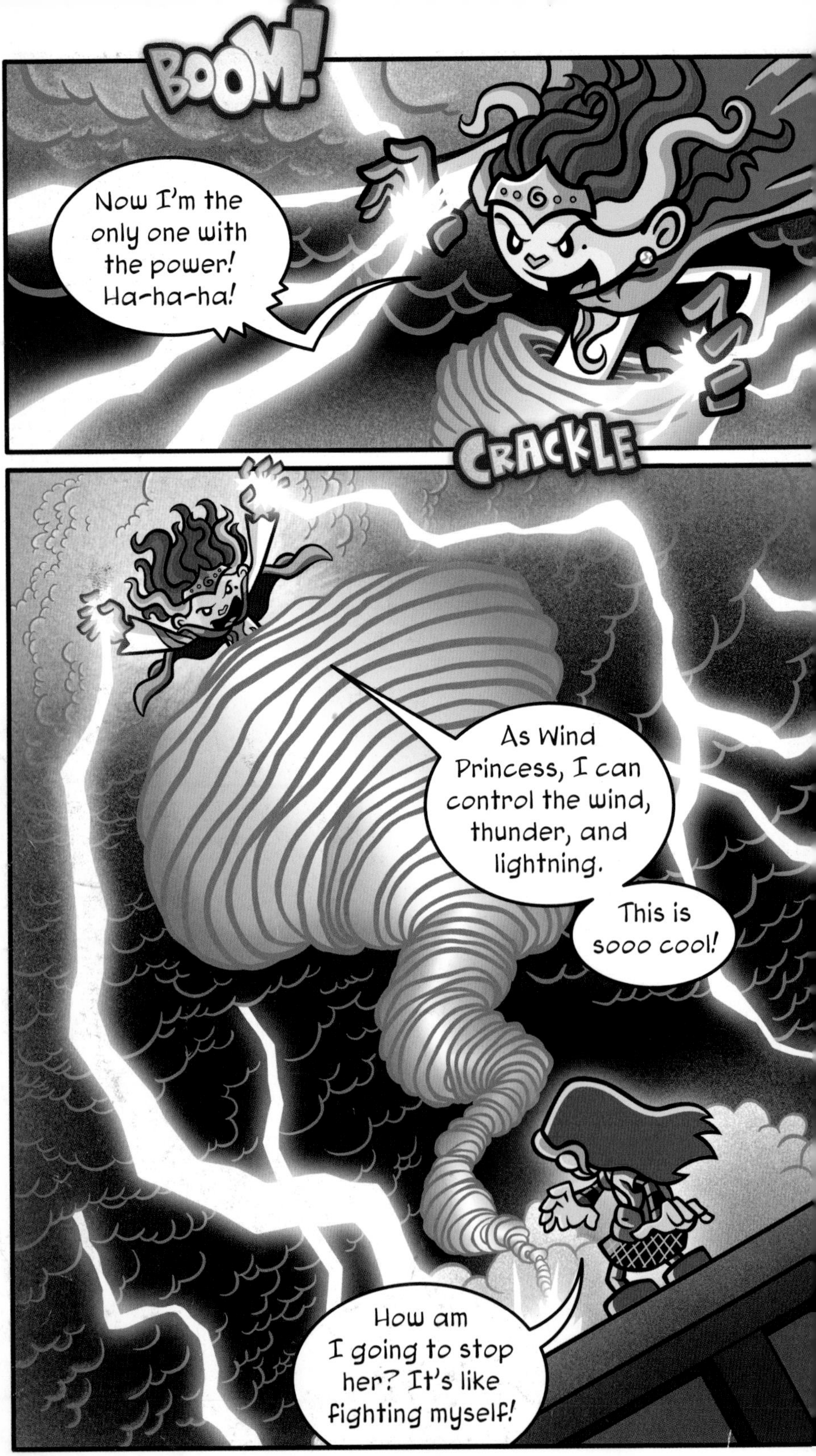
BOOM!
Now I'm the only one with the power! Ha-ha-ha!
CRACKLE
As Wind Princess, I can control the wind, thunder, and lightning.
This is sooo cool!
How am I going to stop her? It's like fighting myself!

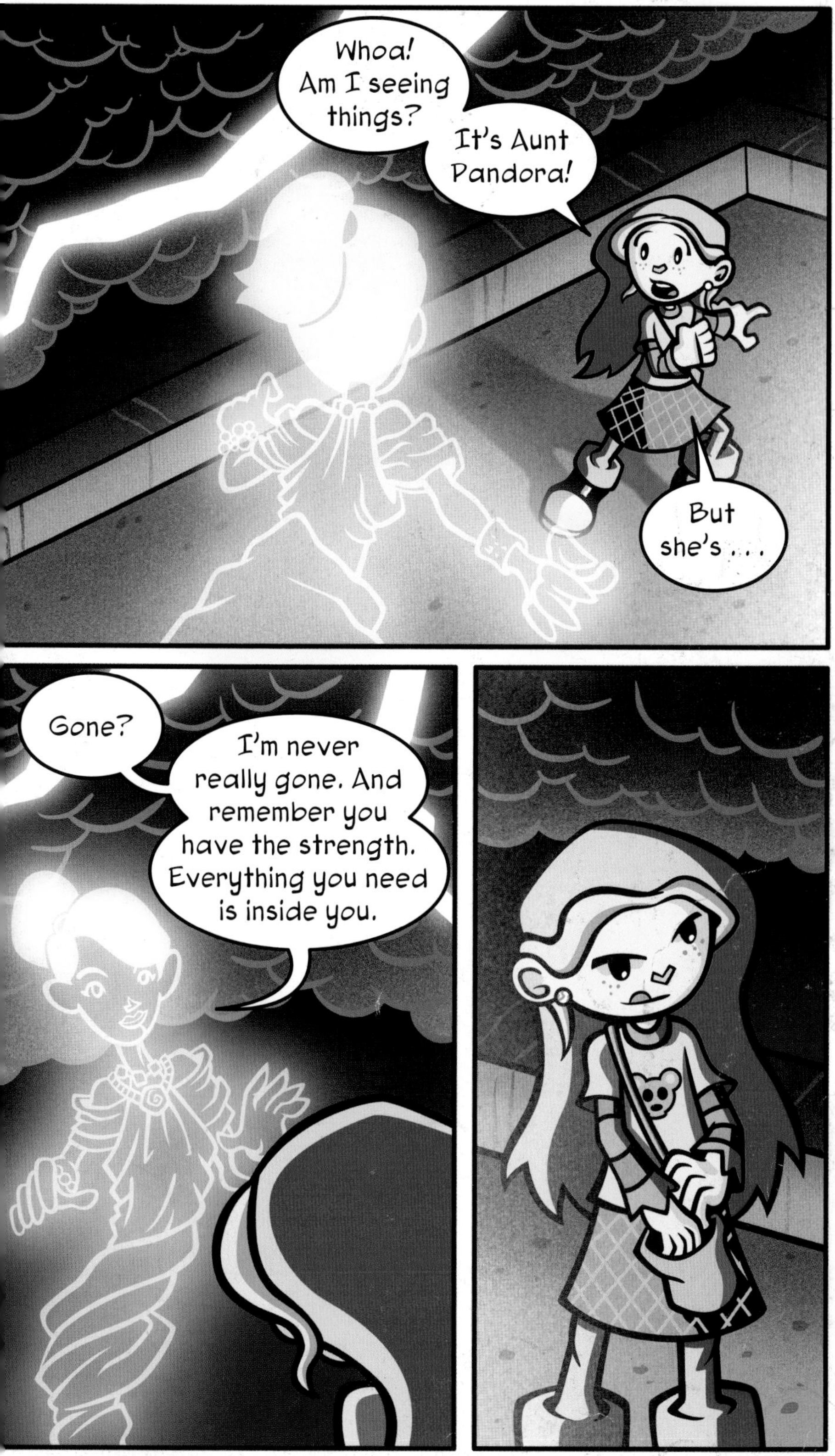
Whoa! Am I seeing things?
It's Aunt Pandora!
But she's . . .
Gone?
I'm never really gone. And remember you have the strength. Everything you need is inside you.

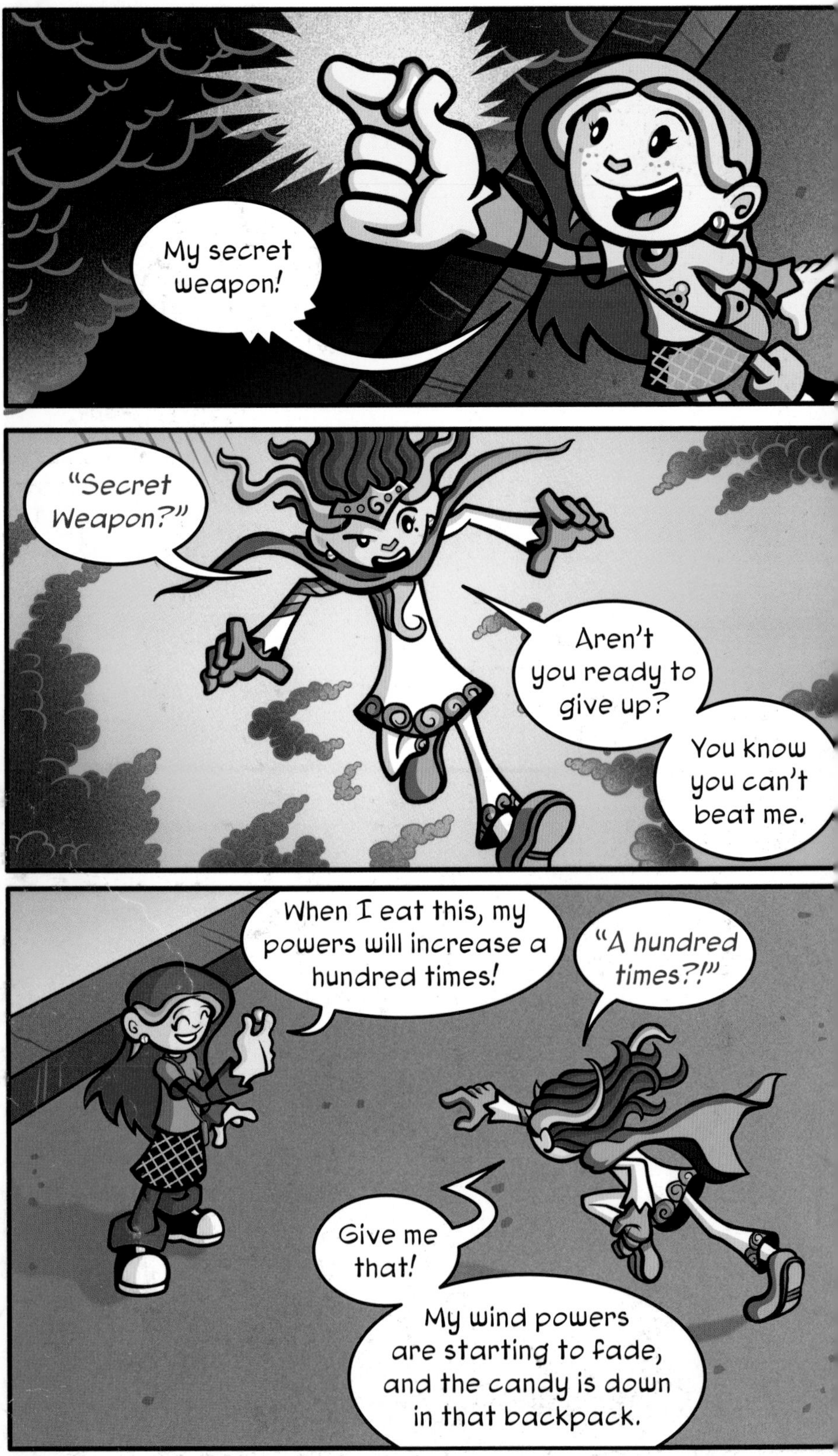
My secret weapon!
"Secret Weapon?"
Aren't you ready to give up?
You know you can't beat me.
When I eat this, my powers will increase a hundred times!
"A hundred times?!"
Give me that!
My wind powers are starting to fade, and the candy is down in that backpack.

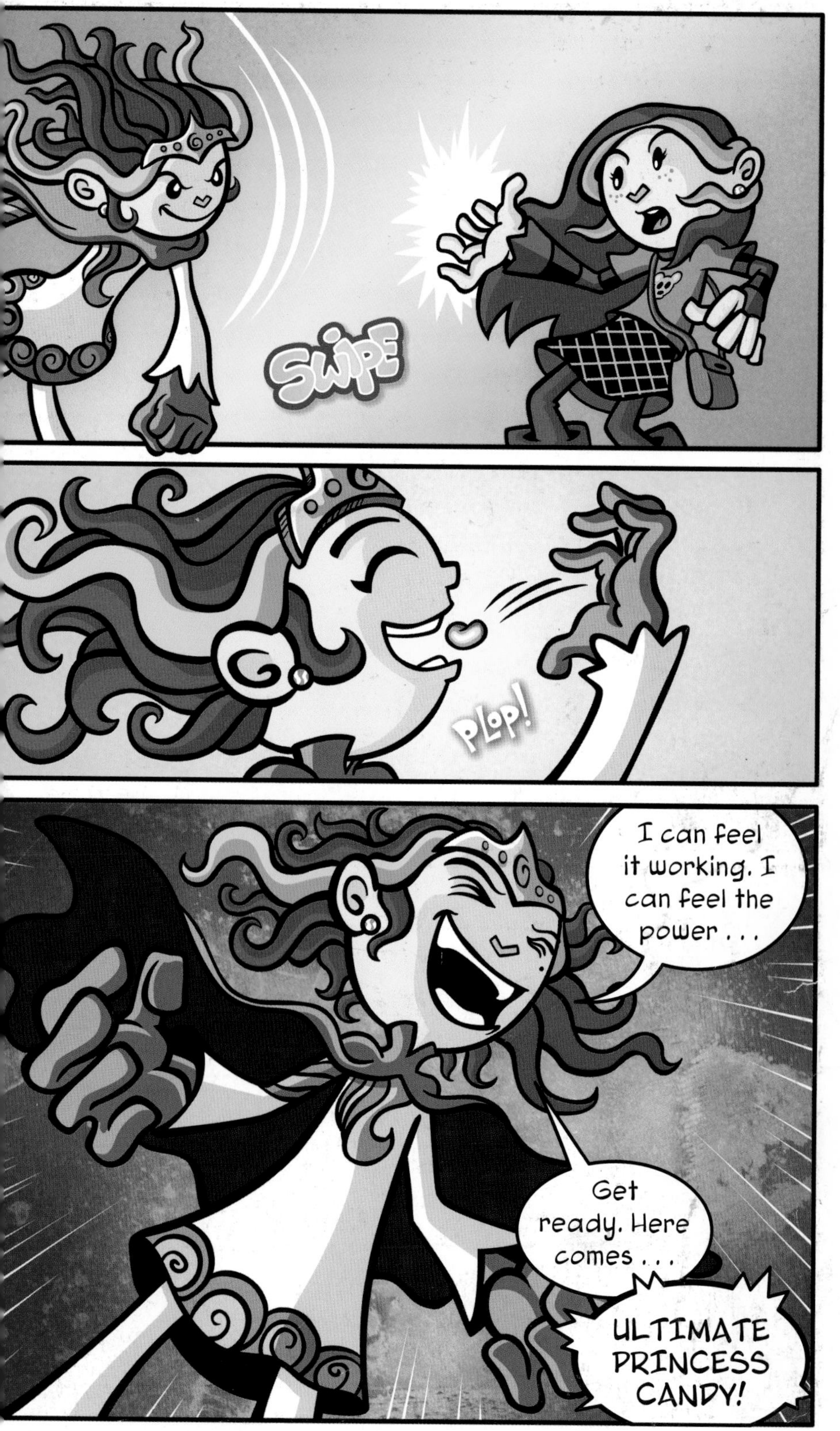
SWIPE!
PLOP!
I can feel it working. I can feel the power . . .
Get ready. Here comes . . .
ULTIMATE PRINCESS CANDY!

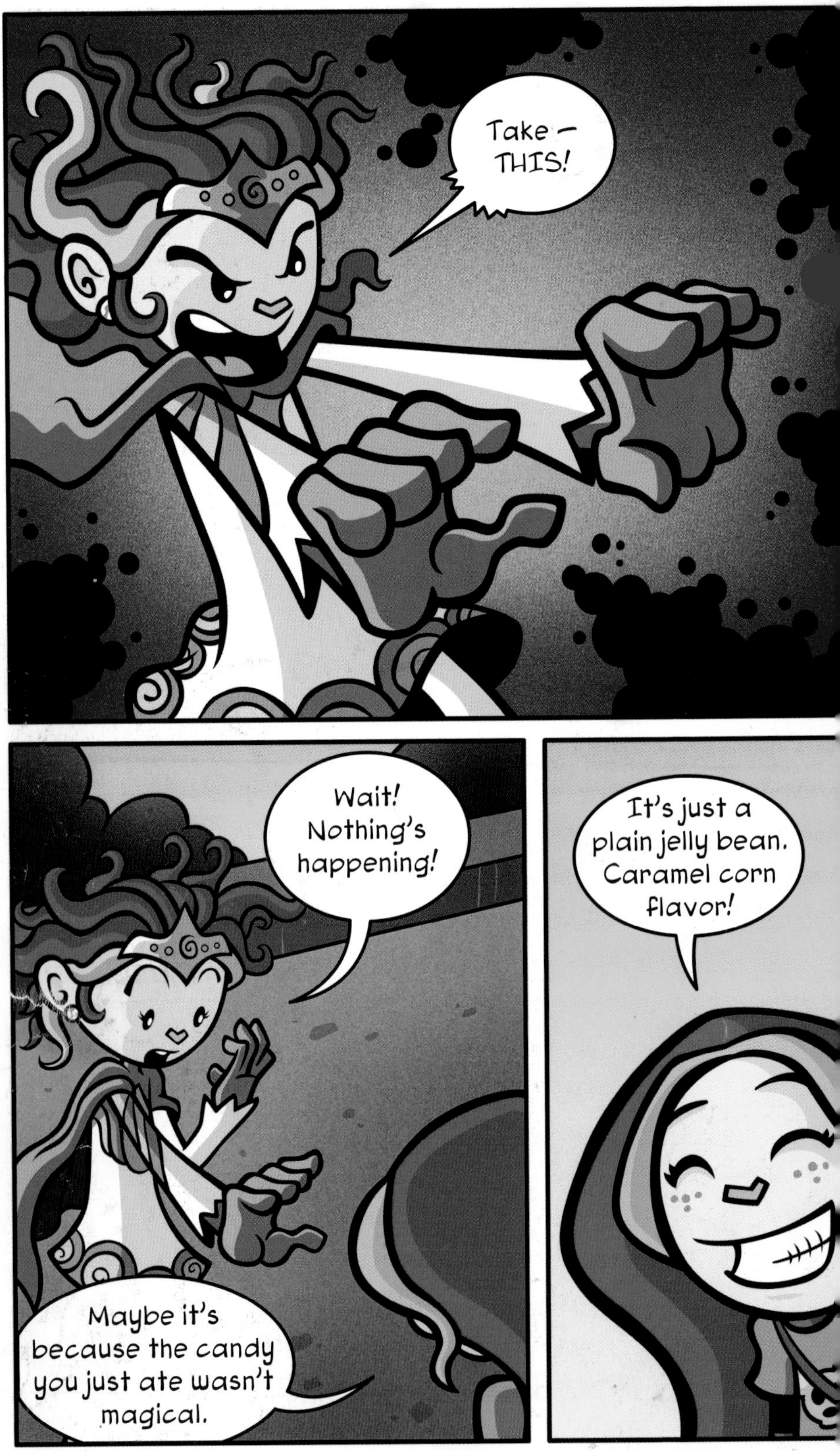

Take — THIS!
Wait! Nothing's happening!
Maybe it's because the candy you just ate wasn't magical.
It's just a plain jelly bean. Caramel corn flavor!

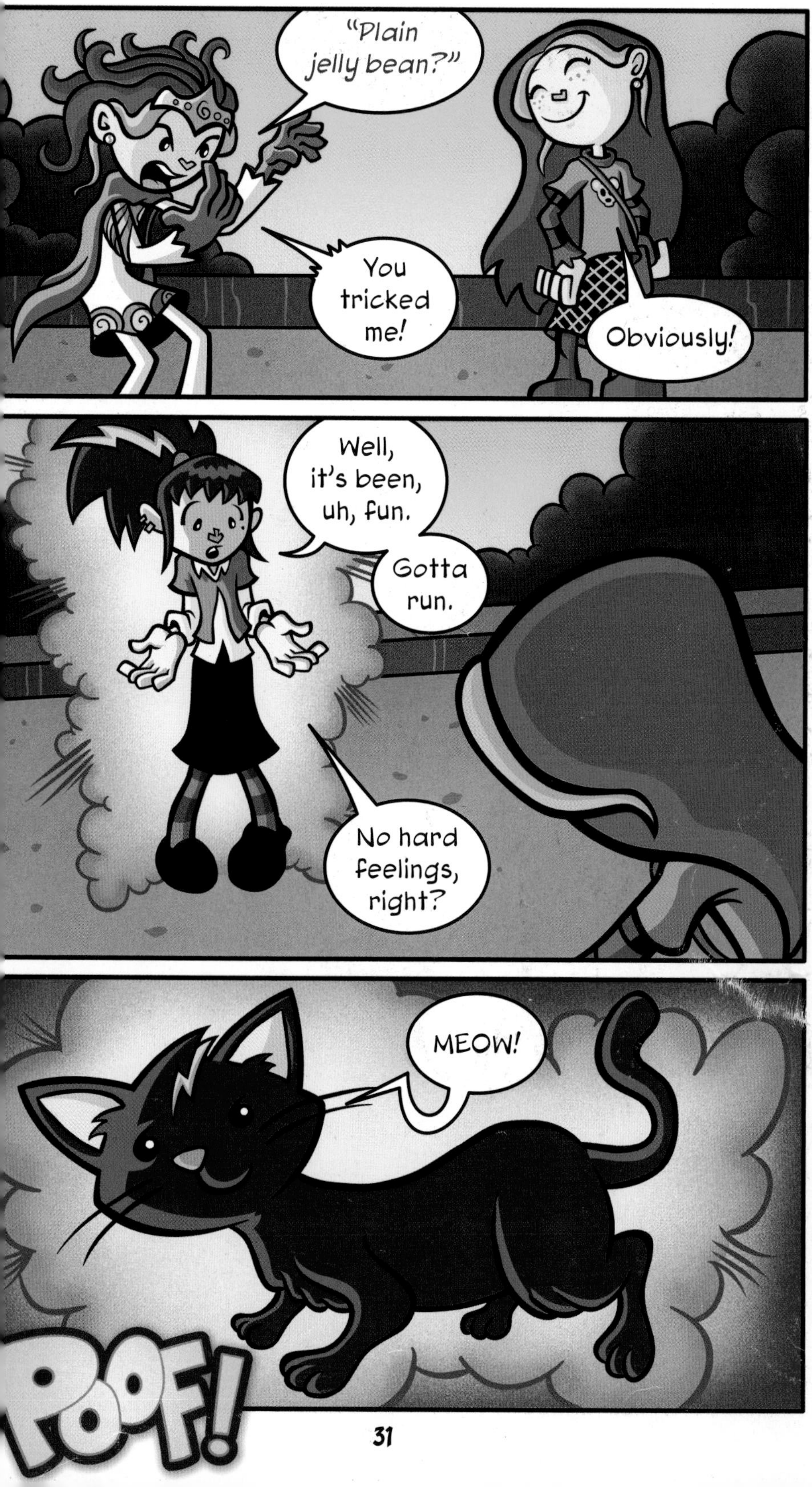
"Plain jelly bean?"
You tricked me!
Obviously!
Well, it's been, uh, fun.
Gotta run.
No hard feelings, right?
MEOW!
POOF!

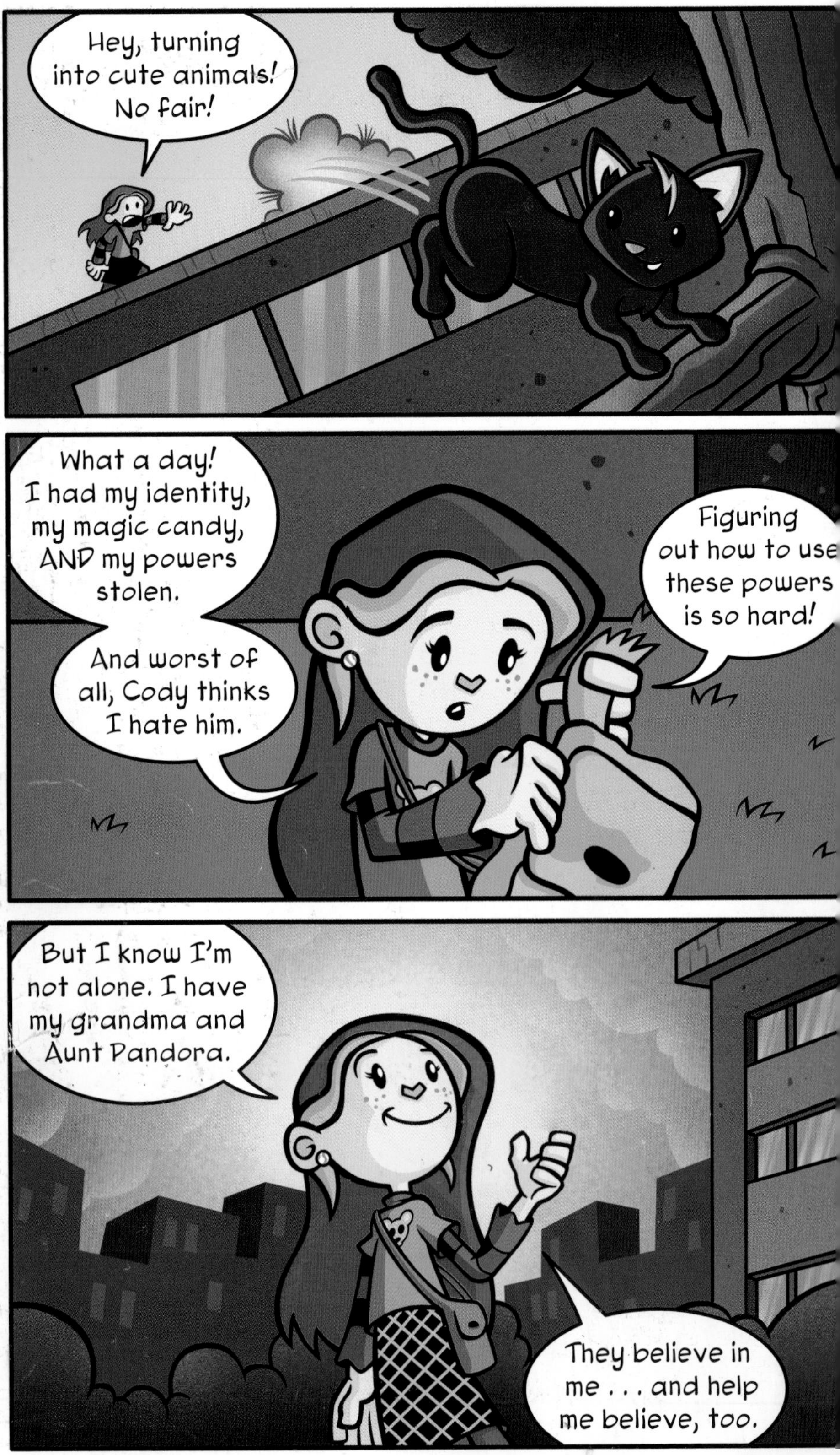
Hey, turning into cute animals! No fair!
What a day! I had my identity, my magic candy, AND my powers stolen.
And worst of all, Cody thinks I hate him.
Figuring out how to use these powers is so hard!
But I know I'm not alone. I have my grandma and Aunt Pandora.
They believe in me . . . and help me believe, too.

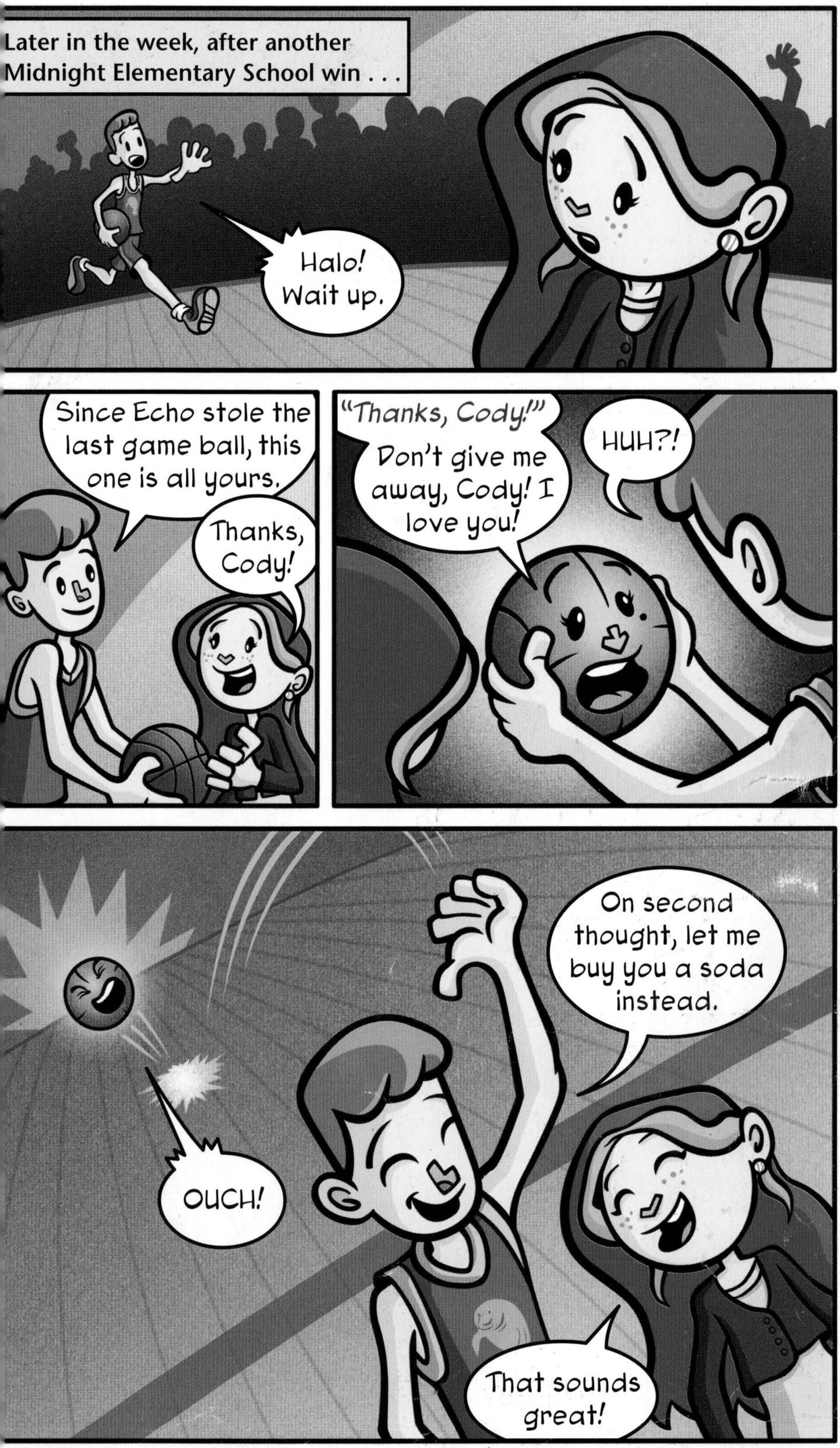

Later in the week, after another Midnight Elementary School win . . .
Halo! Wait up.
Since Echo stole the last game ball, this one is all yours.
Thanks, Cody!
"Thanks, Cody!"
Don't give me away, Cody! I love you!
HUH?!
On second thought, let me buy you a soda instead.
OUCH!
That sounds great!

Evil Echo

SUPER-VILLAIN

Villain Facts

First Appearance
Princess Candy: The Evil Echo

Real Name.......................Echo Repeater

Occupation................................Student

Height.............................4 feet 8 inches

Weight...................................76 pounds

Eyes..........Varies, depending on shape

Hair..............Varies, with green streaks

Special Powers
Repetitive speech patterns annoys all
who hear her; can shift shape into
whoever or whatever she wishes.

Kelly and Kelli Repeater had always dreamed of having twins. So when their
daughter Echo was born an only child, they were shattered. To cope with their
disappointment, the Repeaters taught Echo to repeat phrases. It made the
young parents feel like they had a precious pair rather than a sad singleton.
When Echo was five, her parents' dreams finally came true, and Echo had
twin brothers. Feeling more alone than ever, Echo discovered she could shift
shapes. Now Echo can be a twin to anyone or anything she chooses. She does
not hesitate to over take others' lives, leaving a mess in her path.

PRINCESS PUZZLERS

Q: When were jelly beans invented?

A: In the 1880s.

Q: How long does it take to make a Jelly Belly jelly bean?

A: One to three weeks, depending on the flavor.

Q: How many jelly beans are produced in the United States for Easter each year?

A: More than 16 billion.

About The Author

Michael Dahl has written more than 200 books for children and young adults. He is the creator of Princess Candy and author of *Sugar Hero* and *The Marshmallow Mermaid*, two other books in the series.

Scott Nickel works at Paws, inc., Jim Davis's famous Garfield studio. He has written dozens of children's books, including Princess Candy's *The Green Queen of Mean*, *Jimmy Sniffles vs The Mummy*, and *Secret of the Summer School Zombies*. Scott lives in Indiana with his wife, two sons, six cats, and several sea monkeys.

About The Illustrator

Jeff Crowther has been drawing comics for as long as he can remember. Since graduating from college, Jeff has worked on a variety of illustrations for clients including Disney, *Adventures Magazine*, and *Boy's Life* magazine. He also wrote and illustrated the webcomic *Sketchbook* and has self-published several mini-comics. Jeff lives in Boardman, Ohio, with his wife, Elizabeth, and their children, Jonas and Noelle.

Glossary

arctic (ARK-tik)—extremely cold and wintry

funnel cloud (FUHN-uhl KLOUD)—a cloud that is wide at the top and narrow at the bottom; funnel clouds often become tornadoes

identity (eye-DEN-ti-tee)—who a person is

increase (in-KREESS)—to grow in size or number

magical (MAJ-i-kuhl)—having power that can make impossible things happen by using charms or spells

obviously (OB-vee-uhss-lee)—in a way that is easy to see or understand

powerful (POU-ur-fuhl)—having great strength

strategies (STRAT-uh-jeez)—clever plans for winning a battle or achieving a goal

ultimate (UHL-tuh-mit)—greatest or best

weapon (WEP-uhn)—something that can be used in a fight

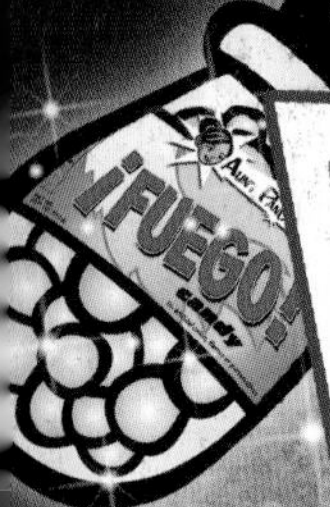
¡FUEGO!
candy

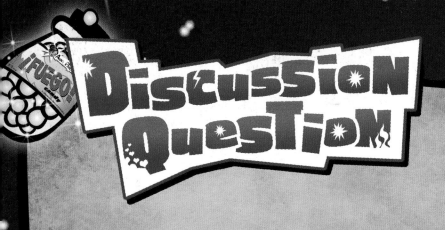

Discussion Questions

1. Early in the story, there were clues that Echo was shape shifting and causing trouble. What were the clues?

2. If you could shift shapes, who or what would you become first? What would you want to do in your shifted shape? What would be the best part of being someone or something else?

3. Aunt Pandora tells Echo, "Everything you need is inside you." What does this mean? Do you think this is true for yourself?

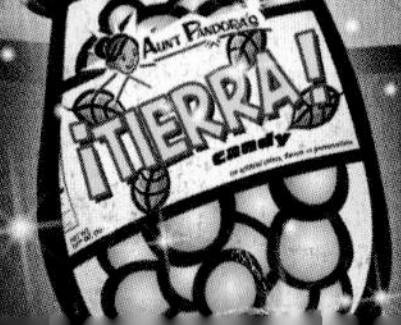
AUNT PANDORA'S
¡TIERRA!
candy

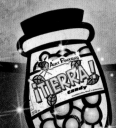

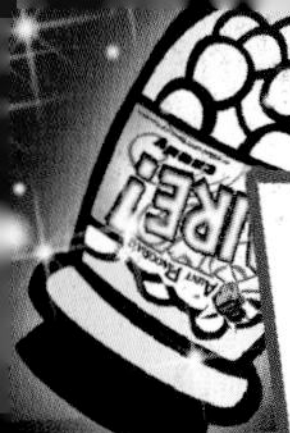

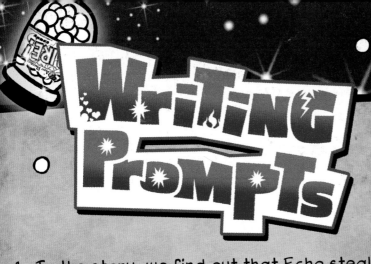

WRITING PROMPTS

1. In the story, we find out that Echo steals Halo's candy. Write a story that shows Echo sneaking into Halo's room. How does she do it? What does she see? What is she thinking?

2. You are a journalist who has been assigned to write a story about mysterious events at Midnight Elementary. Witnesses spotted two nearly identical girls battling each other. Write your news story.

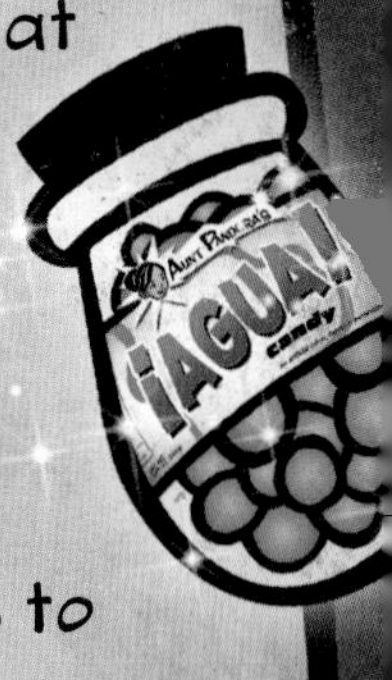

¡AGUA!
candy

3. Writers often use character descriptions to develop their characters' personalities and histories. Write a character description for Echo. Include things about her background, hobbies, and interests.